NOTORIOUS:
Danger, Deception, Desire

TM THORNE

Copyright © 2020 TM Thorne
All rights reserved.
ISBN: 9798645311148

OTHER TITLES BY TM THORNE

FRANKIE FINCH BOOKS

Notorious:
Danger, Deception, Desire

Accused:
Stardom, Scandal, Survival

Driven:
Racing, Rivalry Revenge

Caged:
Rock, Ransom, Retribution

Made:
The Frankie Finch prequel (short story)

THE LONDON VAMPIRE SERIES

Spooked

Jinxed

Enthralled (short story)

ABOUT THE AUTHOR

TM Thorne lived in London for many years before giving in to property prices and the demands of raising a family, and now lives messily in the English countryside with her motorsport-mad husband and son and three demanding cats.

When not writing about her much-missed city, spending time with her family or tripping over engines and spanners littered around the house she likes to eat, drink and feel guilty about not doing enough exercise.

You can find out more about the author and sign up to her mailing list through social media or on her very own website:

Instagram: Instagram.com/tmthorneauthor
Facebook: facebook.com/tmthorneauthor
Twitter: @tmthorneauthor
Website: www.tmthorne.com

CONTENTS

1	Business as Usual	1
2	The Lesser Spotted Frankie Finch	9
3	A New Challenge	15
4	Eyes on The Prize	20
5	Uproar & Ultimatums	28
6	The Morning After	33
7	Getting Rid of Frustration	38
8	Tantrums & Turnarounds	44
9	A Black Eye & A Warm Feeling Inside	47
10	Hot-headed & Hungover	49
11	Glitter & Desire	51
12	Black Cabs & Casting Sofas	59
13	Greasy Chips & Confidences	72
14	Bitches & Bonfires	77
15	Scraping the Barrel	84
16	Razzle Dazzle & Diamonds	88
17	Sick of it All	94
18	First Contact	96
19	Hollywood Hustle	107
20	Rules of Engagement	112
21	Death in the Family	123
22	A Delicate Standoff	131
23	Introductions & Insecurities	134
24	The Happy Couple	145
25	A New Beginning	147
26	Not the Best Start	151
27	Taking Care of Business	157
28	Scrambled Eggs & Champagne	159

29	Coppers & Cake	163
30	Butterflies & Blushes	167
31	It's Been Emotional	171
32	A New Experience	174
33	That's a Wrap	181
34	Regret & Retaliation	187
35	Opportunities & Inconveniences	192
36	Going Loco	196
37	Stepping Up	202
38	Counterattack	209
39	Ruin & Rock Bottom	212
40	Let's Dance	214
41	Hollywood Reboot	216
42	Albanian Girl	218
43	Scissors & Sirens	225
44	Tea & Tough Love	229
45	Death & Divorce	233
46	Endings & Beginnings	237

Copyright © 2020 TM Thorne
All rights reserved.

This book or any portion thereof may not be reproduced or used in any matter whatsoever without the express written permission of the publisher except for the use of brief quotations in book review.

This is a work of fiction. Names, characters, businesses, places, events and incidents are either the products of the author's imagination or used in a fictitious manner. Any resemblance to actual persons, living or dead, or actual events is purely coincidental and unintentional. Even when recognisable names appear, their actions are fictitious.

1
BUSINESS AS USUAL

Ivy saw Clay's eyes light up and she suppressed a sigh. Following his gaze, she realised why she'd lost his attention—new prey. A woman with long dark hair spilling over her shoulders had just walked into the club. She was pretty, wearing a glittery cream cocktail dress. *A bit obvious,* thought Ivy, *but that was just his type.*

Poor unsuspecting thing. Ivy couldn't decide whether to pity or envy the woman. After all, if Clay succeeded in charming her, she would have no complaints. When he lavished his attention on someone, it felt glorious, but like a supernova, his interest burnt out all too soon.

She chewed her lip as she wondered whether Clay would pay her more attention if she glammed herself up, but quickly dismissed that idea. She didn't want to be discarded the way those women were. They may have his undivided attention for a few hours, it may be a night they'd remember fondly, but that was all they ever got.

Ivy watched as the woman made her way across the room, eyes wide with excitement as she clutched her boyfriend's hand, for all the good that would do. A boyfriend wouldn't stop Clay, not once he had his sights set on her. She'd seen this scenario unfold all too often before.

Like a hawk, Clay focused on the woman who was chatting and giggling, taking in the exotic surroundings complete with fountains, the famous flamingos and of course the night sky above which made this London's leading rooftop nightspot.

Ivy gave a small shake of her head and went to serve a customer. As she mixed a gin and tonic, she glanced back over but knew she'd lost Clay for the evening. Why did she put herself through this?

Smiling automatically, she placed the drinks on the bar and was left once again to her thoughts. She leaned her elbows on the countertop. Clay was bad news; she knew that. He wasn't a bad person; he just had a short attention span and an eye for the ladies. His head was always turned by a pretty face, but despite that, she didn't seem able to walk away. She couldn't help but wonder - would he always be content with one night stands and easy conquests? Or would he one day want more, to settle down? She let out a breath. She had to face facts. If she were going to be the one to tame him, it would have happened years ago. She needed to move on and get a life that didn't revolve around him, stop being such a doormat.

Clay was one of those guys who seemed to have everything, a perfect life, but it hadn't always been that way. His real name was Clarence, but only his mum called him that. Some of the boys in the club nicknamed him Pardon after an incident left him with part of his ear missing and a wicked scar which ran the length of one side of his face. Despite this, he was easily the best-looking man in the club and had a smooth charm which he used to great effect to keep punters happy and the club a top London party venue.

He was dressed, as always, in a sharp suit, the cruel scar highlighting the beauty of the rest of his face and giving him an edge of danger, enough to remind people that this place was owned by the notorious Frankie Finch and they were in gangster territory. Beautiful, opulent gangster territory, but gangster territory all the same. This wasn't a place to start a fight.

Not that anyone minded. The lure of partying in such luxury with an added glimpse of the underworld was part of the club's appeal, and the tables were full night after night. The typical customers had steady jobs and were bored with their everyday lives, to which The Flamingo Club added some longed-for spice.

Clay was happy to deliver. He had a natural ability to make everyone feel special; he remembered people's names, had an excellent memory for faces, and just five minutes of conversation with him could make someone's evening and raise the mood of a group.

The same effortless charisma also made him a hit with women, and when he focused his undivided attention on a girl, she invariably fell under his spell. Ivy should know.

The doorman knew Clay's tastes well and must have let the couple skip the queue. Big Arf had been in his job since the club was a snooker hall and was well-schooled in who got special treatment and who was left standing out in the cold. Towering over most people at an impressive 6ft 9, Big Arf wasn't a man to mess with. Although that never stopped Clay, who joked he was called Arf because he only had 'arfa brain, much to Ivy's annoyance. He might not be the sharpest tool in the box, but Big Arf was one of the sweetest men she'd ever met. Unless you broke the rules of course, then you saw a very different side to him. His job was simple, but he did it well. He unclipped the velvet rope for the rich and well-connected and held back the regular people as they shivered in their gladrags outside. And of course, he managed any trouble and kept an eye out for pretty girls and let them skip the queue.

And now Clay had scented tonight's quarry.

Ivy had known Clay forever. They'd gone to school together, and she was one of the few people who knew him before he got his scar. They'd even dated for a while at school, and he'd been her first, something she'd never quite been able to leave behind, but which had just been the start of an extensive list of conquests for him. Perhaps it wasn't surprising with the parade of beautiful women flaunting themselves in front of him every night.

Someone moved into Ivy's eye line, and she looked up.

"Seriously girl? Are you mooning over him again?" said Clementine, hands-on-hips.

"What? No, I was just lost in thought."

Clementine wasn't fooled. She reached over and tucked a stray strand of Ivy's auburn hair behind her ear; a gesture so affectionate that it took the bluster out of Ivy's sails. "So why are you standing there staring at the back of his head then? If you spent less time fawning over Clay and more time chatting to the customers, you might actually find yourself someone nice." Her voice dropped to an excited whisper. "Hey, you'll never guess what, I've just been asked out by none other than Monty Granville."

That got Ivy's attention. Monty Granville, or to give him his full title Lord Montgomery Geraldo Edwin Granville, son of the rakish Stephen Granville, Marquess of Shropshire, was one of the most eligible bachelors in London and following in his father's rather infamous footsteps. Beautiful socialites were practically beating each other with their Birkin handbags in a race to get him down the aisle. His reputation was notorious, but everyone knew he was under pressure to settle down and start producing heirs. Besides, he was very easy on the eye, which made his indiscretions easier to forgive. Ivy nodded, impressed. "Good on you! Nice work!"

"I know, he's taking me out to dinner tomorrow."

Ivy smiled, pleased for her friend. Perhaps Clementine was right. There was no point hanging around hoping that Clay would change his ways. She needed to buck her ideas up. Ivy glanced back over at the unsuspecting couple. They had been sent a complimentary bottle of champagne and looked thrilled. For a moment, she felt a pang of sympathy for the boyfriend. He had no idea what was coming. But Ivy did. She'd seen it all before.

Clay felt a familiar excitement rising as he took a seat at his usual table, the boys budging up to make room for him. The chase had begun.

The couple kept looking over at him. The man had been pleased when the free bottle of champagne was sent over. It made him look important in front of his girlfriend, or so he thought. The woman shot Clay a coy smile, and his eyes sparkled. A lamb to the slaughter.

After a glass or two of champagne for Dutch courage, she nervously approached their table.

"We just want to say thanks so much for the champagne," she gushed, colour blooming in her cheeks. "It's so kind of you!"

Clay gave her a megawatt smile and asked if the two of them would like to join their table. Watching her hurry back, he waited, confident she'd return. When they did, the group parted allowing the couple to slide into the middle of the curved booth: Clay on one side and the boys on the other. They called for a bottle of whiskey, and the man, a little overawed by his new gangster drinking buddies, tried to keep up. He wasn't used to hard liquor, and it wasn't long before he was slurring and laughing too loudly at their jokes.

Meanwhile, Clay concentrated on the woman. She was nervous, twitchy like a frightened rabbit, but with some gentle coaxing, she gradually relaxed. He asked a few probing questions then just let her talk, topping up her glass of champagne and listening. She really was very pretty. He saw a flash of annoyance cross her face as her boyfriend laughed raucously and caught her with an elbow as he told a story. She was having such a lovely time, and he was embarrassing her.

Perfect. Giving her a kind smile, he took her hand and

led her off to dance. She hesitated, unsure whether she should, and glanced back at her boyfriend. But he was seated with his back to the dance floor and was too busy having fun with his new friends to notice she'd gone. Sod him, she thought angrily, and as she and Clay moved together to the music, she softened and leant into him.

Clay took his time, charming her and making her laugh, and they kept dancing as the music became slower and the atmosphere more intimate. He pulled her closer and felt the mood between them shift. This was where the stakes were raised. If she was going to back out and lose her nerve, she would do it now. He kept moving, his hand on the small of her back, her body pressed against his. He could feel the tension between them; the air almost crackling with it. With his lips close to her ear, he whispered: "Christ, you're beautiful". Her breathing was fast and shallow as he dipped his head and laid the lightest of kisses on her neck, making her gasp. Clay glanced over her shoulder at the boyfriend. He looked like he couldn't focus on the men around him, let alone on what his girl was doing.

"Let's get some air," he said, taking the woman's hand. She nodded, eyes wide and serious. But instead of taking her to see the view, he led her through a door marked *Private* and into his office. Closing the door behind them, he pulled her close and kissed her. She melted against him, their tongues softly exploring, a low moan escaping her lips. He slowly unzipped the back of her dress, letting it fall to the floor, his hands roaming across her soft curves. Pulling away, the corner of his mouth twitched as her face creased in a frown. He put his hands on her shoulders and, stepping back, looked at her, her eyes heavy with desire, naked except for panties and shoes. Magnificent.

Liberated by champagne and longing, the woman was no longer the shrinking violet she had been earlier. She'd just needed the right man to unleash the wildness in her. He moved back in, kissing her throat and running his hands over her breasts, eliciting a groan as her head fell back, hair cascading in dark waves behind her. Clay smiled to himself. This was just how he'd imagined her when she'd first walked into the club. Slowly he slipped his hand between her legs. Wet and ready for him. They always were.

The woman fumbled with clumsy fingers to undo his tie and shirt buttons, struggling to concentrate as his fingers worked expertly away, distracting her.

Then he gently leant her back against the desk, the moonlight through the slatted blinds making shadows across her body. Clay paused for a second to appreciate the sight of her, lying there ready for him, eyes bright and excited until he felt her hips move to urge him on. He pushed into her, both of them exhaling raggedly as they drew together. Then he began to move.

Afterwards, they lay panting on the desk, flushed and elated. Clay re-fastened his belt and poured a couple of fingers of whiskey over ice. The woman propped herself up on her elbows, hair tousled and face glowing. Clay took an ice cube into his mouth then, his eyes playful, leaned forward and planted an ice-cold kiss on her nipple. She gasped and closed her eyes, then laughed. He stood back, crunching the ice, his lips pulling into a smile.

"We'd better get you back to that boyfriend of yours before he misses you."

The woman's expression fell as she remembered her abandoned boyfriend. Her hand flew to her mouth.

"Shit, Jerry! I'd completely forgotten about him."

"Well, I would hope you had," smiled Clay slowly. "My feelings would be hurt if you'd been thinking about him this whole time." He ran his lips along her neck again, then pulled her to her feet and brought her in for a long slow kiss, his hands resting lightly on her hips. Releasing her, he slapped her on the bottom with a wink.

"You'd better get dressed sweetheart. The boys won't be able to keep your boyfriend busy forever. You leave first. We don't want him seeing us coming out together. If he asks, say you've just been to the loo. He's had enough to drink that he won't question it."

Clay sank into his leather desk chair, watching as she wriggled back into her dress.

"Shit," she said flustered, "Where are my knickers?" After searching for a few moments, she shrugged and gave up. Now the moment was over, she was feeling anxious. Keen to get back to her boyfriend before he rumbled her. She'd just have to brave the rest of the night without underwear. It was hardly the riskiest thing she'd done tonight. Jerry would be too drunk to notice anyway. And if he did, she'd pretend she'd done it as a risqué treat for him. She opened the door a crack, turning to smile at Clay before ducking out and back into the club.

Once she'd gone Clay put his feet up on the desk and poured himself another drink, pulling her knickers out of his pocket with a grin.

He rested his head back and chuckled. Life was good.

There was a knock at the door, and Ivy appeared, looking worried.

"You'd better get out here Clay. Frankie's just walked in."

2
THE LESSER SPOTTED FRANKIE FINCH

Clay jumped to his feet, shrugging his shirt back on, tying his tie with stumbling fingers. *What the hell was Frankie doing here?* The boss hadn't been to the club during opening hours in over a year now. He would stroll in regular as clockwork every Tuesday morning for a weekly catch-up and a rundown of the accounts, but socially he'd been off the radar for years. Clay was left to run the club his way, and that was precisely how he liked it.

Pausing to check his reflection and smooth back his hair, Clay grabbed his jacket, put his game face on and strolled back out onto the floor as if he didn't have a care in the world. The atmosphere in the club had changed. Frankie arriving had done that.

Like ripples spreading when a stone splashes into a pond, all heads had gradually turned when he walked in. The punters would be delighted they'd shared the same air as the famed Frankie Finch.

There was a time when Frankie had spent every night

at the club, living it up, being the man about town. But not for years now. Ever since the death of his best friend and partner in the business, he'd been seen less and less, almost to the extent that he'd become a recluse. In his absence, Frankie's reputation, strength and reach had continued to expand aggressively, and he'd become a kind of urban myth. Mothers at their wit's end warned naughty children that Frankie Finch would come and have a word if they didn't behave, and so his legend increased.

So it was no surprise that Frankie's appearance had heightened the buzz in the club. People whispered and nudged one another. They would all have something exciting to tell the neighbours the next day.

Clay didn't share their excitement. He wanted a quiet, run-of-the-mill evening with no hassle. An unannounced visit from Frankie wasn't what he'd had in mind. It was bound to mean trouble.

Frankie Finch smiled his shark's smile as he surveyed the club. The place was full, and the atmosphere lively, but he was unimpressed. For starters, he'd been disappointed by the size of the queue out front. Time was, people would queue around the block on the off chance of getting in. The poor mugs would be grateful just to be there, even if it meant spending their Saturday night standing out in the rain. But now it seemed standards were slipping, and that wouldn't do.

He spotted Clay leaving the office, and his eyebrow twitched. No guessing what he'd been up to. He saw Clay wink at a brunette who kept nervously adjusting the hemline of her dress as she tried to manage her drunk boyfriend.

Same old Clay, thought Frankie. *Thinking with his dick as usual.*

Frankie had to admit Clay was a great frontman for the club. That boy could charm the birds from the trees, but all the same, Frankie was starting to question whether he had the business instinct, or the focus, to manage the place going forward.

As he scanned the crowd, his gaze sliding over eager, expectant faces, Frankie's irritation grew. *For fuck's sake! Was he the most famous face in here tonight?*

He'd had a hands-off approach for too long, this was shocking. He didn't recognise a single face. Where were all the celebs? The rich and famous that used to love this place and keep the regular people desperate to get inside? A club needed magic to be successful, or it became mundane, run of the mill, and that wouldn't do. People would think he'd lost his touch. Every table might be full, but it was clear to Frankie that the club was just ticking over. That needed to change and sharpish.

He glanced at Linda, who slipped her hand into his. She looked lovely tonight, a little tired and anxious maybe, but perhaps that wasn't surprising. Their baby boy had been born three months ago, and still wasn't sleeping well. What with that and having a strident four-year-old tearing up the place she was run ragged.

Frankie felt a night out would help. So, to Linda's reluctance, her mother had been drafted in to babysit. And while Linda had agreed that a change of scene would be welcome – a much-needed escape from the same four walls, dirty nappies and the banality of baby groups - she looked like her head was still at home.

The incident with Ron was nearly five years ago now, but it had had a lasting effect on both of them. Linda had never fully recovered; as if she expected another tragedy to be lurking around every corner.

Frankie kept her out of his business dealings as much as possible, but after Ron's death, she was so jumpy he'd made an exception. He'd taken her to one side and assured her that the threat had been eliminated. Totally and irreversibly eliminated. And after that, she appeared to relax, and life went back to normal, or so he thought.

But with the birth of the baby, all her anxiety seemed to

resurface. He gave her hand a squeeze and saw her make a conscious effort to shake off her frown. She slapped on her brightest smile. *That's it love,* thought Frankie proudly, *fake it till you make it. You're the boss's wife, chin up, shoulders back, play the part.* She'd find it easier as the evening went on and she got back into the swing of things.

There was a time they'd both loved this place. The Flamingo Club was Frankie's flagship business, and they had both been so proud of it. But things had soured once Ron was no longer there to run it with him, and the place just served as a reminder of everything Frankie had lost. So he handed the day-to-day running over to Clay. It held too many painful memories, which was why he was so angry to find the place sliding into a decline.

After Ron's death and the disappearance, or more accurately the decimation, of the rival Dixon family who were responsible, Frankie had needed to keep busy. Which was handy since he had his plate full consolidating his new position in the massive power vacuum he'd created.

The Dixons had been a stabilising, if unpleasant, force in East London and their sudden absence left a gaping hole that needed filling. The last thing Frankie wanted was a neighbouring gang stepping up and causing him a headache. He'd had to recruit and expand fast. Not a bad thing as he needed the distraction. Whenever he had five minutes to stop and think his mind filled with doubts about his past actions and their consequences, and he started seeing invisible threats around every corner.

So Frankie threw himself into work. The Dixons, for all their faults, had supplied goods and maintained order in the local area, the responsibility for which now fell on Frankie's shoulders, especially since he was unwilling to share. He worked furiously to stop anyone else muscling in on his new territory.

Consequently, ever since he'd been on constant alert, putting down anyone who wanted a piece of the action for themselves. He'd been ruthless and given no second chances. The Dixons had managed the lion's share of narcotics coming into East London, and Frankie could ill afford for someone else to take that on, they would gain too much power, so Frankie had stepped up.

The only part of the defunct Dixon empire that Frankie left alone was their chain of seedy knocking shops. He generally kept Linda out of the business, after all, the less she knew, the better, plausible deniability and all that, but she had laid down the law on that one. She was happy to turn a blind eye to what was going on unless it involved him hanging around scantily clad women who tempted him to sample the merchandise. She'd seen enough episodes of *The Sopranos* to know that never ended well.

Frankie hadn't argued. He had enough on his plate without getting a headache from Linda at home. So the Dixon's lap dancing clubs and brothels had gradually fallen into disrepair or been taken over by other people. Frankie didn't care about the loss of income, but he was uncomfortable with the lack of control. He couldn't afford to let someone else get a foothold, but he had so much else going on that he let it slide.

After the Dixons, he'd needed to expand rapidly, so he'd used a pyramid scheme of responsibility to ensure loyalty, only hiring people he knew well and trusted and expected them to do the same. After all, they would be held to account for the actions of anyone they brought on board. And early on he established that punishments for letting him down would be swift and brutal.

That way he kept things from getting out of control, but it did sometimes feel like he was juggling a dozen balls at any one time, while riding a unicycle on a tightrope, at the same time as having to placate Linda and make time for his family. Frankie's life was far from simple.

On the upside this system allowed him to direct operations from afar, removing himself from any direct involvement with illegal activity. Linda would go mental if he got banged up, and he wouldn't be able to keep them safe if he was inside. On the public face of things, he was a successful businessman, but of course, everyone knew what happened if you crossed Frankie Finch. And he liked that.

Since the club's opening night nearly five years ago he'd opened a string of pubs, chip shops and betting shops across the area, meaning that whatever your vice on a Saturday night, Frankie Finch got to profit from it.

Clay greeted Frankie with a shake of the hand and a warm grin. *Charming as always*, smiled Frankie to himself. *That's why he's paid the big bucks.*

"Good to see you're still enjoying yourself, Clay," said Frankie jerking his head towards the girl, "but I have to say I'm disappointed. This place isn't what it used to be."

"You're kidding me, right? We're full every night of the week!"

Frankie clapped Clay on the cheek and leaned into him. "Don't try it on with me sunshine. This place used to be the hottest ticket in town, and under your management, it's looking like a regular nightclub. We need some headlines, a bit of fucking pizzazz, get some celebs in. This place used to be exclusive. And right now it looks a bit fucking ordinary."

He pressed a finger into Clay's chest. "Get some ideas together, and I want to hear them on Tuesday morning. Tell me how you're going to get this place back on the map again. Or I'll get someone in who can."

"Of course, Frankie. No problem," said Clay, his mind whirring. This was the last thing he needed. He knew Frankie paying a visit would be bad news. Why couldn't he keep his nose out?

3
A NEW CHALLENGE

Feeling nervous was a new experience for Clay. But as the meeting with Frankie approached, he felt a creeping anxiety. He'd been coasting for years, and in his heart of hearts, he knew it. Running the club was his dream job, like being paid to party every night, so Frankie's intervention was a bit of a bombshell.

Thankfully the meeting went better than expected. Frankie was impressed and, to Clay's indignation, somewhat surprised by his show of initiative. Relief washed over Clay, the last thing he wanted was to be demoted to working in a chip shop or stuck out in the cold as a doorman. This was a cushy job, and he intended to keep it.

The genius idea he'd presented to Frankie had come from Ivy.

While Clay had reacted to Frankie's announcement by going into a blind panic and reaching for a drink, Ivy had listened patiently and started thinking. As Clay sat at the bar, getting progressively drunker until he couldn't remember why he was stressed in the first place, she came up with a plan.

That night she'd been unable to sleep for thinking about it as her mind formulated an idea to get Clay out of trouble.

By the following morning, she'd had a brainwave. On the way to work, she walked past a local street where they were filming a big Hollywood gangster movie. It was being shot on location in the East End, and for the past few weeks, the papers had been full of photos of American movie stars eating pie and mash, going to the greyhounds or having a pint in the local boozer.

All that, of course, would have been engineered by publicists, but that didn't matter, local excitement was high, and it was great exposure for the film.

Ivy hung around and got chatting to one of the runners. He confirmed what she'd suspected, that filming was finishing at the end of the week. *Perfect timing!*

She rushed over to the club to talk to Clay, and he'd immediately jumped on board. It was the perfect idea, but would they be able to pull it off? And even if they did, would Frankie agree?

Ivy needn't have worried. Schmoozing and charming people was Clay's forte, and by the time Frankie strolled in for the Tuesday morning meeting the two of them had pulled off a bit of a coup.

Film director Ezra Swartz, a small, bearded American who adored everything British, had been immediately smitten with Clay. That scar, paired with his angelic face made him perfect for a cameo in the movie. He was the real deal, a genuine East End pretty boy gangster. So when Clay offered to host a wrap party at the club, a club owned by the famous Frankie Finch, Ezra had been easily persuaded. After all, it would be great publicity for the film, and even he'd heard of the infamous Flamingo Club.

Frankie was delighted by the idea. Clay had offered Ezra private hire of the club for the night free of charge (which Frankie wasn't so impressed about), but since they'd be paying for all their own drinks and the press would have a field day it would more than pay for itself in bar takings and publicity.

Clay made a mental note to call a few photographers and give them a heads up to ensure maximum coverage. He was no film buff but even he'd heard of Hollywood bad boy Tyler Wilde and knew he was guaranteed to generate column inches.

Once Frankie gave his seal of approval, Clay breathed a sigh of relief. Now there was just the small task of getting ready for the party, which was only a few days away. He called in his assistant manager, a mild-mannered young man called Stanley, and told him to order in extra champagne and to come up with some ideas to make the club look spectacular. Then he poured himself a drink and leaned back with his feet on the desk. Crisis averted.

Clay's shoulders slumped as a new text dinged on his phone. Ezra was real excited about his real East End gangster party and kept messaging Clay with requests. He now wanted East End canapés for the party. *What the fuck were East End canapés?* This idiot was starting to drive him mad.

He replied with a thumbs up, but in all honesty, had no idea what Ezra was expecting; maybe he could send Stanley out to grab a dozen jars of pickled eggs and some pork scratchings to go on the bar top? That would do, surely? At least it was genuine East End grub. Plus salty bar snacks would make people drink more champagne, and as Frankie had stressed repeatedly, he wanted to keep bar receipts as high as possible to make up for closing to the public on a Saturday night.

Perhaps he'd get some jellied eels and trays of fresh oysters on ice too. After all, Ezra was footing the bill.

He and Stanley hauled out the old red carpet which had been in the back of a cupboard for years and after a great deal of hoovering and steaming, with Stanley doing all the work and Clay watching, it was ready to be laid outside. Once they added some velvet ropes for photographers to stand behind, it would look the business. Clay just hoped there would be enough photographers there to make this worthwhile. It might be a private party but, as Frankie had made clear, he couldn't afford for the event to be a damp squib.

By 7pm, Clay was relieved to see at least a dozen photographers standing out front waiting for guests to arrive. He smirked. Word had got round despite it being a private party, thank goodness for that.

An hour later when still no guests had arrived, and the photographers were getting fidgety, Clay, who was losing his nerve, sent them a tray of complimentary drinks. He needn't have worried; they knew they couldn't afford to walk away. After all, no self-respecting celeb wanted to be the first to arrive.

A murmur of surprise rippled through the crowd as a red London bus pulled up to the pavement. A few of the photographers heckled, shouting at the driver to piss off and park elsewhere. It was only when the doors opened, and a tuxedoed Ezra stepped onto the pavement with the leading lady on his arm that they shut up and sprang into action.

Clay, watching from the doorway, smiled. Nice touch that bus. That had been another one of Ivy's ideas. It had got the paps snapping, and it was in everyone's interests that tonight got into the papers.

Big Arf stood back beside the door, arms folded, his face impassive. But he was enjoying himself. He loved a big celeb event and had a front-row view as the cast left the bus one by one to walk the red carpet, stopping and posing for the bank of photographers.

Tyler Wilde sauntered down the carpet, looking like a fashion model and gave the paps a winning grin. Clay felt a wave of irritation. *Fucking poseur.*

The greatest stir came when a striking platinum blonde stepped off the bus. She wore a daring red satin dress, which skimmed and clung to her voluptuous curves. It was slit to the hip on one side and dipped down so low at the back that it revealed the curve of her lower back and a tiny star tattoo.

Wow, thought Clay, *now that's a woman. No, not a woman, a goddess.* And just like that Clay forgot about the rest of the event. He knew what, or rather who, he would be doing that evening.

The photographers went crazy. It was a breezy evening, and the woman laughed as she struggled to maintain a little modesty as her slashed scrap of a dress was taken by the breeze. Clay grinned a predatory grin. All of a sudden, he was looking forward to this evening.

4
EYES ON THE PRIZE

Pandora bathed in the sea of camera flashes; she was in her element. She didn't care about the wind catching her dress; in fact, it was perfect. If anything was guaranteed to get her the front page tomorrow, it was a flash of knickers or a cheeky nip slip.

As she laughed and blew a kiss at the photographers, Ezra watched her from the doorway, and she smiled at him. Once the photographers were satisfied, she scampered inside and gratefully accepted a glass of champagne. It tasted delicious and calmed her nerves. She had a lot of networking to do tonight. This was her first movie role and, even though it was only a small part, she planned to maximise her exposure and launch herself a proper movie career.

While Pandora's role was incidental rather than major, she'd made the most of her five minutes on screen. Cast as the mistress of a gangster, she was only in two scenes, but she'd made sure every second counted. In the first she seduced the mob boss, played by none other than Tyler Wilde, so that had been no great hardship. And the scene where she performed a slow striptease for him was, in Ezra's words, sensational. So good even that he'd promised to put a clip of it in the trailer to tantalise audiences.

Her second scene was later as the victim in a retaliation killing by a rival gang. The script had called for her to be shot in the face, but she'd convinced Ezra it would be better if she were found in her underwear shot through the chest. Playing a sexy murder victim was going to be so much better for her career than having her face blown off in a gruesome mob murder.

Until now Pandora's career had been limited to TV work and modelling, but now she'd had a taste of the big time she was hungry for so much more.

She wanted to be a star and was more determined than ever to make that happen. She'd just shot her first calendar which was being released to coincide with the movie publicity. Thinking of the risqué photos, she smiled grimly. That would give her stuffy parents a shock. She'd done more than flash a bit of cleavage in those pictures.

She took a sip of champagne and looked around the room. Ezra wiggled his fingers at her, and she went over to join him. He was definitely someone who could open doors for her.

Clay leant back against the bar, eyeing proceedings. Once the guests were in, and the doors were shut on the photographers, the cast and crew could relax. They'd been on a punishing work schedule for the past few months and all needed to blow off some steam. Little did they know Frankie had another photographer poised waiting to capture any action that happened, even if it was for his own private leverage, but that wouldn't be until later once they'd all loosened up.

Once Clay was satisfied that the guests were settled, the drinks were flowing freely, and everyone was having fun, he turned his attention back to the girl in the red dress.

He knew exactly where she was, of course. His eyes kept being irresistibly drawn back to her. She was getting plenty of attention, not least because every time she sat down the slashed dress parted exposing her long tan legs. He wondered how they would feel wrapped around him later and smiled to himself. She'd been keeping a hand in her lap the whole time to stop the dress from gaping too much, but as she relaxed, she was beginning to forget. As the guy sitting next to her had noticed, judging by the way his gaze kept darting back to the area between her legs.

Clay felt a thrill of excitement. He couldn't wait to get her alone.

He heard a raucous cheer and turned to look over at the source. His lip twitched in annoyance. It was Tyler Wilde's table making all the noise, a group of men all focused on a girl who seemed to be peeling her clothes off. That was fine with him. He was glad Wilde's attention was firmly away from his girl. He didn't want to have to compete with that tosser for her attention.

Just then Ezra spotted Clay and called him over. He was still enamoured with his real cockney gangster, and he insisted Clay join them.

Clay allowed himself to be persuaded; this was his perfect opportunity. Pandora looked at him with appraising eyes when he pulled up a seat next to her, and he made a monumental effort to not glance down into her lap or at the expanse of leg that was on display. He gave her a warm sexy smile and then turned back to Ezra. He couldn't afford to look leery; she must get that from guys all the time. He needed to play it cool, to be different to all the salivating fools that hung around her like flies around a honeypot.

So Clay concentrated his attention on the whole group, telling wild stories and making everyone laugh, charming as ever, but remaining intensely aware of the woman sitting only inches from him.

There were eight people around the table including

Ezra and to his right the formidable Vivienne Sinclair. The older woman and leading lady had pulled out all the stops tonight, showing every bit of her Hollywood pedigree. The diamonds she wore dazzled as they caught the lights, and when she smiled that oh-so-famous-smile, even Clay was enchanted. She had once been the hottest name in Hollywood, but that was twenty years ago now, and while she was still a very attractive woman, her career was starting to fade. She no longer got the sexy love-interest roles, those all went to girls like Pandora, and Vivienne hated her for that.

Clay made an effort to spread his attention equally, and after a while, he sensed Pandora relax as she decided that perhaps he wasn't only there to try and pick her up and they started to chat. But despite her initial wariness, they could both feel the attraction between them.

As the evening progressed, the dance floor filled, and the night sky above them twinkled with stars. It was a warm night, and a slight breeze rippled the leaves of the palm trees as the hum of the city sounded below them. It was a perfect evening.

And it was the perfect time for Clay to make his move. The music was now loud enough that they were struggling to hear one another so, leaning over close enough for her to feel his breath on her neck, he murmured, "Come and dance."

He saw her shiver, and she gave him a slow smile. She got to her feet, but as she did the creep to her left – the one who had been leering at her crotch all evening - grabbed her arm. He was a pale man with close-cropped hair and the sweaty sheen of someone who'd had too much to drink.

"Hey 'Dora," he slurred, "Don't go! We haven't had a chat yet."

She laughed as she firmly removed his hand from her arm. "I'm only going for a dance, Steve. A girl's allowed to have a little fun."

Steve didn't agree, and as she got to her feet, he grabbed at her dress to pull her back. There was a terrible ripping sound as the thigh split, which had already been daringly high, tore right up the front nearly splitting the dress in two. Pandora gasped and clasped the ripped fabric back together, horrified, but Clay was already on his feet. He grabbed the guy by the scruff of the neck and dragged him, scrabbling and whining, over to the doorway before throwing him down the stairs.

"Get this creep out of here," he growled to the security guard lurking in the hallway.

He turned back to the room hearing Vivienne's tinkly laugh as she enjoyed the moment, and felt a flash of annoyance. His eyes scanned the club, but Pandora was nowhere to be seen.

Clay looked questioningly at Ivy who rolled her eyes in exasperation and pointed to the toilets. Clay strode off in that direction.

Not pausing, he walked straight into the Ladies to find Pandora in tears, hugging the tattered dress around her. He frowned. *Had no one come after her? Were they all so self-obsessed that they'd just gone back to partying?*

She gaped at him. "What the hell are you doing in here? Get out!"

Clay ignored her and shrugged off his jacket, placing it around her shoulders. She gratefully slid it on and wrapped it around herself. She inhaled deeply, relishing its comforting warmth and scent of his citrusy aftershave.

"Come on," he said, offering his hand, "let's see if we can get you sorted out."

"I'm not going back out there."

"It's OK; you don't have to."

She sniffed and regarded herself in the mirror. She looked a state. Dabbing away the makeup smeared under her eyes, she allowed him to lead her out. After all, she couldn't stay in the toilets all night, and the last thing she needed was for bloody Vivienne Sinclair to come and find her in here. The superior bitch would love that.

To Pandora's relief, they didn't head back into the club but instead went through a door marked 'No Entry', taking them to Clay's office. He opened the door and ushered her inside, his heart rate quickening in anticipation. It wasn't how he'd planned to get her in here, but it would work just as well.

He moved over to the desk and opened a drawer producing a box of safety pins. Being the manager of a club, you had to be ready for any eventuality, although he'd never foreseen this. He stood before her.

"Let's have a look at the damage then." Pandora hesitated then let the jacket fall open, exposing the jagged slash in the dress which had exposed her stomach, the underside curve of her breast, and the tiniest pair of red lace knickers. Clay's heart raced as he sank to his knees and gently pulled the two pieces of fabric together. Her skin smelled of warm vanilla.

"Hold still," he murmured.

Starting at the top of the rip, he gently pulled the two sides of fabric together and pinned it, her skin breaking into goosebumps as his thumb brushed her stomach. He moved onto the second pin. She held perfectly still, so he didn't catch her with it. She hardly dared breathe. As he came to the fourth pin, he leaned in and placed a gentle kiss on the lowest part of her stomach, just above the thin band of lace, and heard a gasp escape her lips. He continued to pin the fabric together. Pandora watched him with heavy-lidded eyes, the humiliation of earlier now forgotten, as she thought about nothing but this man and how his hands would feel against her skin.

She stayed unmoving, her breath shallow until he was done. Her dress now pulled back together in a jagged scar. She almost laughed at the crazy patch-up job, but she didn't want to break the moment. Clay rose to stand in front of her, finally meeting her gaze. They regarded each other for a long moment before she reached out, taking hold of his tie and slowly drew him in until his lips were tantalisingly close. They paused, breathing one another in, then he closed the gap. Their lips met, and it was like a fire igniting.

As the kiss deepened and became more urgent, there was no hesitation, no holding back. Pandora pressed herself against Clay; his hands and lips seemed to be everywhere. There was another tearing as the pinned fabric gave way, but they both just grinned and carried on, not caring. This time though the tear went all the way, the dress splitting in two and hanging to either side. Clay thought he'd never seen anything sexier.

As he lifted her onto the desk, he kissed down her neck to her exposed breast. He watched her response, her back arching, legs wrapped around him, a moan escaping her lips.

She was every bit as magnificent as he'd hoped.

Just then there was a sharp rap at the door. They both froze, and Clay put a finger to his lips, hoping whoever it was would go away, but the knocking persisted.

"Clay?" hissed Ivy, "You need to get out here now, we've got a situation."

Clay blinked slowly. He looked at Pandora and whispered, "Don't move."

He opened the door a crack.

"What? This had better be good."

"It's Frankie. He's just walked in, and he's not happy. You'd better get out here."

Clay exhaled slowly and pinched the bridge of his nose.

"I'll be right there," and he closed the door again. He turned back to Pandora, who was looking dishevelled and unbelievably sexy on the desk. He shook his head. *Great fucking timing, Frankie. This had better be important.*

He kissed her again, his hand running briefly between her legs. She was so ready for him. He groaned in frustration.

"I've got to go, but I won't be long, promise. Wait for me?"

She looked up at him with those big green eyes and nodded, biting her lip. And with great reluctance Clay headed back out into the club.

5
UPROAR & ULTIMATUMS

Clay walked out onto the floor and couldn't believe his eyes. All hell had broken loose.

There was a scuffle underway by the bar, the raucous men were snorting cocaine off the now-naked woman, Tyler fucking Wilde was balanced on the balcony pissing into the street below, and a couple were getting hot and heavy against one of the palm trees.

How the hell had this all happened since he'd been gone? Clay looked desperately over at Ezra wondering why he hadn't maintained some control, only to find him with his face buried in the unbuttoned blouse of a young woman as she enthusiastically massaged his crotch. Clay winced as a dropped bottle of champagne exploded scattering glass shrapnel all over the floor and startling the usually unflappable flamingos. Amidst the mayhem, he spotted Frankie, standing stock still looking thunderous.

Clay's heart sank. *Frankie chose the worst moments to turn up.*

He spoke quickly into his earpiece calling the security guards up from the door to help him regain control. Then, striding over to Wilde, Clay grabbed him by the belt and dragged him back off the balcony wall, dumping him unceremoniously on the floor. Wilde roared in outrage, but Clay didn't care. Better to make the guy angry than have him kill himself falling from the balcony.

Straightening his tie Clay approached the furious figure of Frankie Finch. He paused to yank apart the couple against the palm tree, the girl squealing in response as she quickly righted the skirt that was up around her waist.

"Take it outside," Clay growled, pointing at the exit.

He reached Frankie, shaking his head.

"For fuck's sake, Frankie, what's wrong with these people? They're animals! We don't get this on a normal night. These Hollywood types are a fucking nightmare."

"Perhaps if someone had been keeping an eye on them, the situation wouldn't have got so out of hand."

Clay held up his hands.

"Hey, I was only gone for five minutes while I sorted out another crisis."

Frankie raised an eyebrow as he spotted Pandora slipping out of the office. She'd ditched what remained of the red dress and was now just wearing Clay's suit jacket and a pair of heels.

"She'd be your crisis then would she?"

Clay swore gently under his breath; she hadn't waited for him. Then again, who knew when he would have got back to her with all this kicking off.

"It wasn't like that, Frankie; some joker tore her dress. I lent her my jacket to cover her up."

"Well, that's been effective," said Frankie dryly. The jacket only just covered her bottom, and being single-breasted it dipped to her navel. She looked great, but it left very little to the imagination. How that was an improvement on a ripped dress, Frankie didn't know. Both of them watched as she joined a group by the bar.

Suddenly their attention was caught by a commotion on the other side of the room.

"Help! We need a medic over here!"

"Fuck," muttered Clay, "Is that Tyler Wilde, who looks like he's overdosing?"

"Call an ambulance," barked Frankie who decided it was time he took charge of the situation. Clay had well and truly fucked it up. He strode over towards the man who had slumped onto the floor, a crowd forming around him. *If you want something doing properly…*

He gestured to the band to cut the music, and as silence fell, the atmosphere shifted, like the lights coming on at the end of a school disco. Everyone stopped what they were doing and stood blinking as they tried to get their alcohol-fuddled brains to work.

"Right, you," Frankie said, pointing to the naked cocaine girl, "get your fucking clothes back on. Everyone else, if you've got drugs on you, flush them now. An ambulance is on its way, and the police won't be far behind. So unless you want to spend a night in the cells, get rid of it now."

There was a scramble for the toilets as self-preservation kicked in and the group abandoned Wilde unconscious on the floor.

Frankie shook his head. *Great mates,* he thought, crouching and feeling for the guy's pulse. He couldn't find one, but then he wasn't sure he was doing it right. His job rarely called for first aid skills. *Where the fuck was that ambulance?* The last thing he needed was a drugs death in his club.

Clay paced the pavement outside, directing people towards a fleet of cabs, and looking for the ambulance. Time moved slowly. Frankie would have his guts for garters if that idiot died. Clay couldn't believe how quickly a great evening had descended into an unmitigated disaster.

The ambulance arrived fast, but even so, the club had emptied by the time the paramedics reached the roof garden. Only a few of Tyler's more loyal friends remained.

After ringing 999 Clay's next call had been to a local cab firm, getting them over to the club to spirit the celebs away before word got out. There were bound to be a few lurking photographers, and an ambulance would bring the press back out in full force. No one would want to be papped leaving once word got out about a major A-lister overdosing. Being photographed on your way into a glamorous wrap party is one thing, being associated with a seedy drugs death is quite another.

Sprinting up to the club ahead of the paramedics he pointed them towards the guy on the floor. Tyler Wilde looked like a bad wax effigy of himself, grey and pasty. Clay stood back while they got to work.

Arms folded, his mouth in a grim line, he stood beside Frankie and offered up a silent prayer that the guy would survive. *It had to be a good sign that the paramedics were working frantically on him. At least they were trying, so there had to be hope, right?*

As they loaded Wilde onto a stretcher and took him away, Clay let out a small breath. At least they hadn't pronounced him dead on the spot. The guy was a knob, and probably deserved to overdose, but Clay needed him to pull through. Not least because of the shitstorm that would otherwise unleash. At least there was hope. After all, he hadn't died on the floor of the club.

Clay pulled himself out of his thoughts and looked around. The place looked a state.

He jumped as he felt a hand grasp his shoulder and turned to look up at Frankie.

"Well," Frankie said, voice heavy with sarcasm, "that went well, didn't it?"

Clay shrugged, unsure what to say.

"You'd better get this place cleaned up. I'll be in tomorrow afternoon, and I'll want to know how the hell this happened on your watch. Get it sorted," and he smacked Clay round the back of the head.

"Yes, boss," said Clay.

As soon as Frankie stalked out, Clay walked glumly over to the bar and slid onto a barstool. Ivy poured him a whiskey, and he tacitly downed it. She poured him another.

"What a night, eh?" He gave a humourless chuckle, shaking his head.

"How was Frankie?"

"Pissed off."

"Oh, dear."

"I know. He wants a meeting tomorrow. I can't wait for that."

Ivy's mouth tightened in sympathy, and she put a hand over his.

"Come on, let's get this place cleaned up and call it a night."

Clay looked up at her with a sad smile. She always had his back.

"What would I do without you, Ivy?"

She gave him a wry grin. *Go home with someone else?* she thought, but kept it to herself. Usually so self-assured, Clay looked deflated, and she hadn't got the heart to kick him when he was down.

She left him nursing a bottle of whiskey at the bar, head in his hands and marshalled the rest of the staff to get the place sorted out. She began wearily collecting glasses and stacking them on the bar. There was a lot to do before they could call it a night.

6
THE MORNING AFTER

When Clay woke the next morning in Ivy's bed, his head was pounding. It took him a few moments to recall the events of the previous night, and when he did, he closed his eyes and groaned. Glancing over at Ivy, he winced. She was gently snoring; her red hair spread like a halo over the pillow. He didn't want to wake her; she looked too peaceful.

He slipped back into his clothes and tiptoed downstairs, coming face to face with Ivy's mum in the hall.

"Morning, Clarence," she said disapprovingly.

"Morning Mrs P," he replied chirpily, kissing her on the cheek and pinching a piece of toast off her plate before heading to the door.

Ivy's mum shook her head. That boy was a charmer, but he was a wrong-un. Ivy needed to stop waiting around for him. *Why couldn't she find herself a nice boy who'd treat her right rather than wasting her life being at Clay's beck and call?*

On the way back to his flat Clay stopped to pick up the

morning papers. He needed a hot shower and a strong tea with plenty of sugar before he tried to gauge how the meeting with Frankie would go.

Sadly he couldn't avoid the headlines. The rack of newspapers increased the sense of dread growing in the pit of his stomach. The first tabloid screamed: *Wilde Nights! Tyler's Brush With Death at East End Gangster Coke Party.*

Clay picked up the paper and read on.

Hollywood A-lister Tyler Wilde was rushed to hospital after a drug overdose at Frankie Finch's notorious Flamingo Club last night. The party ended in disaster after Wilde was seen snorting cocaine off the bodies of naked women in a debauched drugs buffet.

Clay ran a hand over his face. *Where the hell had they got that from?* One of the guests must have leaked the story to make themselves a few quid. Or perhaps it was a jealous co-star trying to burn Wilde's career. If he survived, that was. The fact that they weren't reporting his death had to be a good thing.

He took an armful of papers over to the counter.

"Good night?" Chuckled the newsagent, nodding at the headlines.

Clay laughed. "You could say that."

It was kind of funny. Or it would be if he weren't getting the blame for it all. His stomach lurched, and he bolted back out onto the street. Taking a few gulps of fresh air, he pushed down the feeling of foreboding at the thought of his meeting with Frankie. After all, he hadn't done anything wrong.

Frankie was a reasonable man; he'd see that.

Frankie was due in at midday, but despite Clay rationalising the situation, he was still feeling anxious. Whatever Frankie's verdict, he'd just rather know his fate. The unknown was far worse than anything Frankie could do to him. Or at least he hoped it was.

Unable to settle at home, Clay was sitting in his office with the morning's papers spread over the surface of his desk when Frankie strolled in. He jumped to his feet, nearly upending a mug of tea. Frankie wasn't due for another half an hour. Thank Christ he'd got in early!

"You know I should fucking fire you for that fiasco last night?"

Clay said nothing and waited for the axe to fall. He knew better than to interrupt an angry Frankie, not if you wanted to salvage anything positive from the situation.

"I'm tempted to put you on toilet cleaning duty and hand over the club to Stanley."

Clay's eyes narrowed, that was a low blow. Stanley had been eyeing his job for a long time. That little sneak had just been waiting for him to mess things up.

"You've always had an eye for the ladies. I've always known that and that's your business. But when that starts to interfere with the running of the club, it becomes my business. It can't carry on."

Clay nodded. *Where was this leading?*

"If I hear of anything happening that I'm unhappy with you'll be out on your ear, you understand? I'll have you scrubbing piss-stained toilets in every pub in East London for the foreseeable future."

Clay breathed a subtle sigh of relief, Frankie wasn't going to sack him after all. He allowed himself to lean back a fraction in his chair.

"Thanks, Frankie. I know it all went tits up last night, but at least we got some good coverage for the club." He ventured a cheeky smile. "And after all you wanted headlines..."

Frankie raised an eyebrow, then snorted with laughter.

"We certainly got those, didn't we? You're damn lucky that idiot pulled through."

Clay's eyes widened, Wilde must have recovered. That was why Frankie was letting him off. They'd got lucky. From now on, he'd have to be careful though; he couldn't afford another slip-up. He tuned back into what Frankie was saying.

"After last night the police will be keeping a keen eye on this place. I need you to ensure everything is squeaky clean till they relax. I can rely on you for that, can't I?"

Clay nodded. "Yes, boss."

Frankie picked up the brashest of the tabloids and chuckled softly. "You dodged a fucking bullet last night Clay and somehow accidentally pulled off a PR coup. From now on, you take no risks, and I want you on top of everything. And I don't mean our female clientele."

He stood, and Clay scrambled to his feet. "I suggest you tighten security for tonight. After this hitting the news we're going to have people queueing round the block. They'll all want to see where Wilde OD'd, but we can't have any incidents. In the meantime, I'm off to talk to our friendly Detective Inspector. He wants some reassurance there won't be any other drug issues in the club."

He opened the door, then turned, pointing a finger at Clay.

"I mean it; I want this place running like clockwork. No more disappearing off every time a pretty girl makes your dick twitch. Understand?"

"Absolutely, Frankie. Hand on heart."

As the door shut Clay slumped back in his chair, relief washing over him. He was still the king of the club. *Thank Christ for that.* He could have lost it all. He closed his eyes and let out a measured breath before pouring himself a tot of whiskey. His hands were trembling. Now his nerves were calming he realised he was starving. He hadn't eaten since the stolen piece of toast first thing, and he needed a proper breakfast.

Clay glanced back down at the papers, his eyes drawn to a full-length photo of Pandora in that red dress, laughing, knickers flashing as a breeze caught it. She looked sensational and had been responsible for a lot of the more positive headlines. He ran a finger over the photo, a gleam in his eye, as his thoughts returned to the previous night: the way she'd responded to him, the feel of her skin, the taste of her lips. If only they hadn't been interrupted.

He had a lot to do today before they opened and couldn't afford to get distracted, but now he was out of danger Clay felt rising anticipation. He knew she'd come back to the club tonight. After all, they had unfinished business.

7
GETTING RID OF FRUSTRATION

Frankie spent the next hour providing the portly DI Aiden Hunter with a generous portion of saveloy and chips and assurances there wouldn't be any more drug activity in his club. After which he needed to get rid of some frustration.

Controlling his temper didn't come naturally to Frankie, but this was all part of cutting it as a respectable businessman. The rules were a lot more constraining than they had been as a young kid with nothing to lose. He felt locked in a straitjacket made from people's expectations and petty values, and sometimes just wanted to let rip and roar at the world.

There was, however, one place he could still vent his anger, and he was on his way there now.

He knew he'd gone easy on Clay, and as he drove, wondered whether he'd done the right thing. It had been such a relief to hear Wilde had pulled through, was that why he'd let Clay off so lightly? Or was it sentimentality? He'd known Clay forever, and never had any illusions about the boy's weakness for a pretty face. But he was usually damn good at his job. Clay's easygoing charm had proved a real winner in the club and was partly what kept the place successful.

Of course, he'd threatened to replace Clay with Stanley if he fucked up again, but that was an empty threat. Stanley was a great behind-the-scenes man, he kept things running like clockwork, but he was no frontman. If Frankie was honest, Stan was a bit of a goody-two-shoes, a bit too eager to please. And that made Frankie's skin crawl. He liked a man with some self-belief, even if that did sometimes lead to more trouble. And he suspected punters would feel the same. Stanley, for all his conscientiousness, was a wimp.

Still, Frankie was pissed off. He couldn't afford to give the police a reason to come sniffing around. He had a delicate arrangement with local law enforcement where they left him alone as long as there was no trouble in the area, and he didn't draw any attention to himself. A prominent drugs death in one of his clubs might have been too much to turn a blind eye to.

Frankie thought of Ron and wished for the millionth time his partner was still there to talk to. Ron would have known what to do; he was always so sure of everything.

He shook himself angrily. There was no point moping over spilt milk, or spilt blood for that matter. He had no choice but to sort this out himself. Clay had better pull his finger out. Frankie had worked hard and lost a lot to get where he was today and no one, no matter how long he'd known them, could be allowed to jeopardise that.

Most men would feel intimidated walking into Kings Boxing Club, but Frankie was not most men. This place was a home away from home for him. It wasn't one of those namby-pamby gyms you join to shed a few pounds and wear lycra; this was a serious fighters gym that he'd been using since he was a kid.

Frankie had been one hell of a boxer before he'd diversified. It was only when he opened the club five years ago that he stopped fighting competitively. He had an impressive record, and a formidable right hook, and made a mint from both professional and unlicensed bouts. That was how he got the money together to get his businesses started in the first place. He didn't fight any more, at least not in the ring, but he still enjoyed rolling up his sleeves and getting stuck in, especially when he was angry.

"Frankie!" shouted the trainer with his twenty-Marlboro-a-day voice, "be right with you." Del King had run the gym getting on for twenty-five years, keeping local kids off the streets and out of trouble and teaching them discipline as well as how to look after themselves. Frankie had been just a gobby youngster when he first walked through the door, and it was the love for boxing discovered under Del's tutelage that helped him avoid petty crookery and a resulting stint in a young offenders institution.

Del told the kid he was to start doing pushups and came over to shake Frankie's hand.

"You looking to fight today, Frank?"

"Always Del, you know me,"

Del chuckled. Frankie was one of his best fighters; it still frustrated him that he'd retired before he'd reached his full potential. But then he'd gone on to create an empire and cleaned up the local area in the process so he couldn't complain.

"Got anyone good in today?"

Del stroked his jaw as he scanned the room. There were half a dozen men in there, none of whom would be keen to take on Frankie. Most of them had done that and regretted it in the past. As he looked around, they were all busying themselves and avoiding eye contact. They wouldn't turn Frankie down if he asked, but none of them would volunteer to get in the ring with him.

"How about someone new Frankie?"

"You know me, Del. I'll take on anyone. Who've you got for me?"

Del gestured over to a kid who was pounding on the bag. He looked young, 17 or 18 maybe, but he was a big lad. Not meaty, but tall and lean with broad shoulders.

"Come off it, he's just a kid," said Frankie. "I could do with a decent fight, not 30 seconds of dancing then having to apologise to his mum for blacking his eye."

A smile tugged the corners of Del's mouth. "You might be surprised."

Frankie shrugged. What did he care? He'd dispatch this kid then get the next person in the ring. The way he was feeling today, he'd take on the whole fucking lot of them.

As Frankie sat wrapping his hands, he felt his mentality shift, his mind still. He was looking forward to doing something physical. At heart, Frankie was a man of action, and managing businesses all day long left him with a lot of pent-up frustration. He hadn't realised it at the time, but Ron had been a steadying force on him, and he missed having a partner. Now life, despite his success, was a lot more stressful. His mind constantly churned analysing possible threats, only now there was no one to share his concerns with. Clay was the closest thing he had to a second in command, but the idea of sharing his troubles with him was laughable. Clay was too busy thinking with his dick to be of any use.

Frankie was always on the lookout for trouble, a byproduct of growing a business empire in this part of town.

Despite having destroyed the Dixons, he couldn't relax. There was always some joker vying for his crown. Right now he'd got Albanians opening up knocking shops on the edge of his territory who were making him uneasy. They hadn't done anything to prompt him to step in yet, and their brothels and massage parlours were of no interest to him, but he was keeping an eye on them. There were rumours around about them being connected to the Albanian mob. His spider-sense was tingling, and he couldn't shake the feeling that something was about to kick off.

There was also the nagging anxiety about keeping his family safe. Linda wouldn't stand for having what she referred to as 'his goons' in the house the whole time, and after many heated debates, he'd had to concede. She refused to have their lives dictated by what had happened in the past.

"Besides, you dealt with it, didn't you, Frankie?"

He had of course, but being at the top meant there was always someone wanting to take your place. So he kept a couple of his boys stationed in a car outside, just in case.

He took a deep breath, trying to shake off his thoughts, but what he needed was a fight. That would clear his head.

Frankie stepped into the ring, stretching his neck from side to side and rolling his shoulders while Del fastened his gloves. He felt a calm settle around his shoulders. When he was in the ring, it was all about the moment, no thoughts except for his opponent. It was surprising how therapeutic hitting some poor mug could be.

The two fighters sized each other up while Del fussed over them, reminding them of the rules and making sure they were ready. Frankie was confident, but it never did to underestimate anyone. A small crowd had gathered around them, all keen to see Frankie fight now they didn't have to go in the ring themselves. Frankie didn't expect the kid to be on his feet after a few seconds, but he refused to go easy on him just because he was young.

The kid meant business. There was no sign of fear behind his eyes, so Frankie had to give him credit for that. He almost felt bad about the whooping he was going to give the kid, but not that bad.

The two of them moved around the ring, testing each other with a few jabs and blocks. Then Frankie got in a sharp hit to the kid's ribs and was surprised when he didn't so much as flinch. Frankie raised an eyebrow. *OK, perhaps he isn't as green as he looks.* Then the kid ducked and landed a hefty hook to Frankie's jaw, catching him unawares and knocking him on his arse.

The place went silent; everyone waiting to see how Frankie would react. Del held himself ready to step in. *Would Frankie go psycho?* Had he made a mistake putting the kid in the ring with him?

Frankie tasted blood inside his mouth as he sat on the canvas, and his face broke into a crimson grin. He chuckled and got back to his feet. Most people boxed to flatter him. They thought they'd get kneecapped if they didn't keep him happy. This kid was a breath of fresh air.

This was going to be more fun than he'd expected.

8
TANTRUMS & TURNAROUNDS

As evening approached, Clay felt excitement building. He was looking forward to seeing Pandora again. He knew she'd come back to the club and he couldn't wait to carry on where they'd left off.

He went through the motions of getting the club ready to open, but his mind was elsewhere. He left most of the heavy lifting, as usual, to Stanley and Ivy. They had everything under control.

As they reached opening time, Clay changed into a clean shirt and sprayed himself with aftershave before looking at his reflection. He nodded. *Looking good,* he grinned to himself.

Now it was just a waiting game. There was no way she'd be the first person through the door; it just wasn't her style. All the same, he felt impatient. Anticipation was one thing, but he'd already delayed gratification by twenty-four hours, and now the hold-up was driving him crazy.

She'd be feeling the same, so she wouldn't wait too late. And after being interrupted the first time around tonight would be even better.

When, by midnight, there was still no sign of Pandora Clay's occasional whiskey was threatening to turn into a much heavier drinking session.

The club was busy, the atmosphere pleasant if a little more excitable than usual, and as Frankie had predicted the queues had been around the block. But Clay barely noticed. He couldn't think about anything except Pandora.

By the time they closed at 3, he was slouched at the bar with a half-empty bottle of whiskey in front of him. Ivy tried to rouse him from his gloom only for him to snap at her to leave him alone. Clay didn't need her mothering him all the time, and was sick of her fussing around. If he couldn't have Pandora tonight, he didn't want anyone.

Hurt and angry Ivy left the bottle on the bar and got on with clearing up.

Clay didn't notice. He was drunk and couldn't believe the bitch hadn't shown. She could at least have had the decency to return his fucking suit jacket. His frustration growing, he decided he'd had enough of sitting around waiting. She'd made him feel like a fool, and he felt like having a fight.

In fact, what he felt like doing was telling that sneaky fuck Stanley what he thought of him. Clay swayed as he pulled himself to his feet and scanned the room, searching for his target. *Look at him taking over, telling everyone what to do,* he thought sourly, with no thought to the fact that Stanley had been forced to step up because he'd done nothing all evening.

But as Clay moved to give the unsuspecting Stanley a piece of his mind, the alcohol hit him hard, and his knees buckled. Grasping the bar he stood for a moment, breathing slowly, waiting for the room to stop spinning. He didn't notice Ivy, her mouth set in a grim line, as she asked Big Arf to get him outside and into a cab.

There was no way she was going to try and deal with him tonight. He wasn't used to rejection, and he was taking it badly. *Welcome to the real world,* she thought, his unkind words from earlier still stinging.

9
A BLACK EYE & A WARM FEELING INSIDE

Frankie looked in the mirror, and his battered reflection grinned back at him. It had been years since someone had been able to black his eye. He liked that kid Chris. He had balls.

Linda hadn't been impressed, of course. Never known to miss a thing, she'd spotted the deepening bruise on Frankie's face as soon as he'd walked through the door and her expression had immediately soured. She stood, hands-on-hips.

"What the hell have you been up to now, Frankie Finch?"

Frankie smiled and slid his arms around her.

"Nothing to worry about love. I've just been down the gym and got caught unawares, that's all."

Her eyebrows shot upwards. "You're kidding me? Someone gave you a shiner in the ring? You're not losing your touch are you Frankie?"

She wriggled herself free, and Frankie leaned against

the wall watching her arse sway as she went to the fridge and pulled out a steak to put on the bruise.

"Maybe I am," he chuckled. "Hey, you wanted me to give up the fighting. Maybe I'm not as sharp as I used to be. Don't worry. He won't get me next time."

Linda shook her head, but the tension had eased. She'd assumed the bruise was a sign of something worse, some trouble at work. It showed how jumpy she still was. He wasn't sure what he could do about that other than get her some Valium. Occupational hazard really.

But Frankie couldn't worry about that. Besides, he was in a good mood. Sparring with Chris had put some fire back in his belly. It was refreshing to come across someone who wasn't scared of him. Come to think of it, he didn't know why he hadn't seen the kid before; Frankie thought he knew everyone in the local area. Either way, it had taken his mind off his business worries for a while, which was a welcome relief.

He was looking forward to their next bout. He felt something he hadn't felt for years. Excited.

10
HOT-HEADED & HUNGOVER

The next day Clay rose early with sore eyes and a mouth that felt like the Sahara. He staggered to the kitchen to get a glass of water and tried to recall the previous evening. He wasn't even sure how he got home. All he remembered was that Pandora hadn't come back. He took a gulp of water. As it hit his stomach, it turned against him, and he staggered, heaving, for the sink.

Fuck, it had been years since he'd had a proper hangover.

He leant against the counter, trying to catch his breath and wait for the room to stop spinning and wondered why she hadn't shown. *They always came back*. Usually, he ended up trying to get rid of them. No one had ever stood him up before.

Or had he drunk so much he'd missed her? He hoped that wasn't what had happened. He rifled through a drawer looking for paracetamol, refilled his glass and stumbled back to bed.

By the time he woke for a second time, prompted by his

insistent bladder, it was mid-afternoon, and he was feeling better.

He looked as rough as hell, but at least the room wasn't swaying. His headache was more manageable, and he didn't feel like puking any more. In fact, he was starving.

He stood in the shower, turning his face into the stream of water, letting it soothe him, and by the time he emerged, no longer smelling like a wino, he felt like himself again. What he needed now was a fry-up. He'd be as right as rain by opening time.

Fuck Pandora if she wasn't coming back. He didn't need her. There were always beautiful girls coming into the club, and he'd find someone new tonight. But first, he needed a large amount of sausage, bacon, eggs, fried bread, toast and black pudding, washed down with some strong sweet tea.

After that, he'd be back on his A-game. He'd be fucking unstoppable.

11
GLITTER & DESIRE

That night, as Pandora walked into the club, she felt rather foolish. *Would Clay even be there?* She'd thought long and hard about whether to return, the urge to see him warring with the humiliation of the ripped dress incident and that whole disastrous night.

Pandora was ambitious and protected her public image meticulously. She knew her fledgling career teetered on a fulcrum where one bad story could make the industry drop her, and after all her hard work, she refused to slip back into obscurity.

But she'd desperately wanted to return. At the very least to see whether that spark was still there. She'd never felt attraction like it. Had it just been a heady combination of champagne, the occasion and him being a knight in shining armour in her hour of need? Would she feel the same when she saw him again tonight? If he was even there of course. And if it wasn't, at least she had the excuse of returning his jacket to him.

After much persuasion, Pandora's flatmate had agreed to

come along with her tonight. Bea couldn't have been more of a contrast. A sensible girl who was training to be an accountant, she despaired at Pandora's obsession with fame. But she'd listened to her friend fret and obsess about this guy for the last 48 hours, which was unheard of. Pandora was usually pretty detached when it came to men. More focused on her career than on having a boyfriend.

So Bea put on her one going-out dress, a sensible navy shift which served her for anything from a wedding, to a funeral to a rare night out. She'd let Pandora do her hair and makeup and even talk her into removing her round tortoiseshell glasses for the evening, and when she'd looked at her reflection, Bea had been pleasantly surprised. She looked good. Slightly blurry because of the lack of glasses, but good. But then, why was she bothering? Nobody would look her way when she was out with Pandora, who drew stares from every man she passed. Pandora could wear an old sack and still be the most gorgeous woman in the room.

Bea's heart sank as she saw the long queues outside the club. She hadn't brought a coat and was already shivering. Pandora grabbed her hand, pulling her along as she strode up to the front of the queue. Bea shrank back mortified and was surprised when the big doorman winked and unclipped the rope, letting them straight through. There were clearly benefits to going out with Pandora.

When they got to the top floor, they took seats at the bar, Bea gazing wide-eyed at the crowded scene before her. She didn't go out much, preferring a quiet night in and when she did venture out it was to go to the cinema, or a drink at the local pub, so the club was a revelation.

The glamour of it all, the excess, the opulence! She gazed around, soaking in the ambience. Mirrors shone, glasses clinked, the band played, and lights twinkled. Bea hadn't expected there to be palm trees up here, and was that a real live flamingo? She giggled to herself. Pandora handed her a glass of wine, and she took a large gulp to steady her nerves. So this was the world that Pandora lived in?

She leant in to be heard over the noise. "So, which one is he?"

Pandora searched the crowd with a growing sense of disappointment.

"I can't see him. Perhaps he's not working tonight after all."

"I'm sure he would have been here if he'd known you were coming. Let's have a couple of drinks then head home. We might as well salvage something from the evening. It would be a pity to get all dolled up and not have some fun." She paused, her mouth forming a small O as her gaze landed on the figure of a tanned, diminutive man who was sitting at a nearby table with a willowy blonde wearing a dress that probably cost more than Bea's annual salary. She nudged Pandora. "Oh my God, is that Eddy Hewer?"

"Uh-huh," said Pandora unimpressed. "He looks older in real life, doesn't he? It's amazing what a bit of TV makeup can do to smooth over wrinkles, isn't it?"

"His date doesn't seem to mind."

"That's the upside of fame, isn't it? There are always women who want to be with a famous man. He could be vile, but if he's got money, fame and power, there'll always be a pretty face to hang on his arm and heat up his bed."

Bea shot her a sidelong look. Pandora was the most celebrity hungry person she'd ever come across, so that seemed a bit rich. And surprisingly astute. Although, perhaps Bea was doing her an injustice. Pandora was ambitious, yes, but she wasn't the type to do anything to get ahead, she was just really focused.

But the more she glimpsed of this strange world in which Pandora seemed so at home, the more Bea was forced to admit her flatmate's life was a closed book to her.

Pandora spotted Clay in the mirrors behind the bar a few seconds before he reached her. Their reflected eyes met, and she found herself beaming at him.

She didn't turn. Instead, she stayed motionless, holding his gaze as he walked up behind her until she felt a hand slip around her waist. A thrill of pleasure ran through her at his touch.

"Hey," he murmured as their eyes locked on each other. She put her hand on his arm, her heart pounding loudly in her chest as the rest of the room seemed to fade from view.

Oh yes, thought Pandora, *the attraction is definitely still there.* They stood unmoving, caught in one another's gaze before they heard a small cough reminding them that they weren't alone.

"Sorry," said Pandora, regaining her composure, "this is my friend Beatrice."

Clay turned and flashed Bea a winning grin.

"Any friend of Pandora's..." he said, taking her hand and gently brushing the back of it with his lips, causing the colour to rise in Bea's cheeks. "And may I say how ravishing you're looking tonight," he said, giving her a slight bow. Bea smiled back, instantly won over, even though she knew he was only being polite. No, not polite, charming.

Clay snapped his fingers at Ivy, ordering a bottle of champagne. Pandora noticed the girl's mouth tighten. *She likes him,* she realised and looked at the girl anew. She was pretty, in an ethereal sort of way, with a pale complexion and all that red hair, but she wasn't any competition. Reassured, Pandora returned her attention to Clay.

"Come and join me," he gestured to a table in the corner where three young men in sharp suits sat talking and laughing. "I can't leave lovely ladies like you perched on bar stools." And with a chivalrous tilt of his head, which made the girls giggle, he took each of them by the arm and steered them across the room. *Tonight was shaping up to be a much better night.*

Bea clutched her glass of wine, eyes like saucers. She was so out of her comfort zone right now. It was great Pandora had found her guy, who wasn't what she expected but seemed very nice, but now she wished she could go home. Being a third wheel on Pandora's date wasn't her idea of a fun night out.

She'd guessed it might be like this, which was why she'd been reluctant to come, and had been secretly relieved when Pandora hadn't initially spotted Clay, but now he'd appeared she would just have to suck it up. Besides Pandora had promised they'd only stay for an hour whether Clay was there or not.

She slid nervously onto a chair next to a guy with a neatly groomed moustache who turned and gave her a welcoming smile.

"Hello," he said, offering his hand, which Bea shook. "You look wonderful." Bea could feel her colour rising again.

"I'm Stanley," he said as he poured her a glass of champagne. They clinked glasses, and Bea took a sip, scrunching up her face. She'd never tried champagne before, and it prickled her nose.

She smiled gratefully back at him, it was obviously his job to keep her entertained, but that was better than sitting here on her own. She glanced across at Clay and Pandora who were in a world of their own and suppressed a sigh.

Bea was surprised how easy Stanley was to talk to. In his sharp suit, he looked every inch the gangster, although a little softer around the edges, carrying a few extra pounds. They chatted comfortably, and Bea barely noticed when Pandora and Clay got up to dance.

Stanley wasn't what she expected at all. Bea knew the club's reputation, everyone did. It was owned by gangsters. And in his pinstriped suit, this guy looked every inch the part. But he had kind eyes, and she was surprised to discover they had something in common: they both shared a love of going to the movies. They talked about all the latest movie releases, and she was surprised he'd even heard of a new Scandinavian movie she wanted to see.

She looked at him, eyebrow raised. Everything slightly blurry. Was that the champagne or her myopia? She wished she could put her glasses on.

"Do you really want to go and see that film, or are you just saying that to keep me entertained because your boss wants to dance with Pandora?"

He flushed, something she'd never thought a hardened gangster would do.

"No, I totally want to go and see it. Just because I work in Frankie Finch's nightclub doesn't mean I can't like the same things you do."

Bea's eyes widened in horror; she'd offended him. She shouldn't have made assumptions because he worked here. "I'm sorry Stanley, I didn't mean anything by that. I'm just surprised. You live in such an exciting world; I didn't think something as mundane as a Scandi murder mystery would be your kind of thing."

He smiled, "I could prove it to you?"

"Oh yes, and how are you going to do that?" laughed Bea, "Have you got a movie screen hidden away in another room?"

"Not here, silly. Let's go and see it. I think it's on tomorrow night at the Odeon. What do you think?"

Bea didn't know what to say. The last thing she'd expected from this evening was a date. Should she accept? He seemed sweet, but if he worked here, surely he was mixed up with some nasty people. Did she really want to get involved in that world? Then again, it was only one date. And besides, he was asking out of a mutual love of Scandinavian cinema, not because he fancied her. So what was the harm in that?

"OK." A relieved smile spread across his face. Had he been nervous that she'd turn him down? *Surely not?* He poured her another glass of champagne, and they clinked glasses, grinning.

Pandora meanwhile was in turmoil. As she and Clay moved together on the dance floor the rest of the club had faded into background noise. She felt her pulse racing, the faint scent of his aftershave, his body pressed against hers, making her senses reel. They didn't speak. Clay pulled back to look down at her with hungry eyes, and she felt a twinge in response and yearned to kiss him. But she couldn't. Not here. Not in front of everyone.

As if reading her mind, he took her hand, and she allowed herself to be led from the dance floor. Pandora threw a guilty glance over her shoulder at Bea, but she seemed happy enough. She wouldn't notice if they disappeared for five minutes. Well, perhaps ten.

Seconds later, they were in Clay's office once again. Pandora closed the door behind her and turned the key. For a moment, they stood just looking at each other. They'd both wanted this so much; now they were finally alone neither of them wanted to rush things, but still, she couldn't leave Bea alone for too long. Her body aching for his, Pandora closed the gap between them. Her lips paused an inch away from his; she could feel the warmth of his closeness, making her tingle. When he closed the gap, and their lips met, something was unleashed. Their mouths hungry, hands roaming everywhere, desperately fumbling with buttons and zippers to reach the skin beneath.

Pandora hadn't admitted it to herself, but she'd worn her best underwear and a dress she could easily step out of so subconsciously, despite her good intentions, she'd been hoping this would happen. Their clothes discarded on the floor, Pandora leaned against the desk. She felt him bump against her thigh as he kissed her neck. There was no need to prolong things. They'd both been ready for this for two days now. She ran her hands down his back and pulled him impatiently towards her, crying out as he entered her.

They stilled, savouring the feeling for a few brief seconds before Clay began to move. Pandora pushed her hips to meet his, clutching and grasping, all inhibition gone until they crashed to a shuddering climax.

Pandora leaned back on the desk, panting and elated, her skin glowing. Clay grinned down at her, his breath returning to normal. "Sorry," he said. "I couldn't hold back. I just wanted you so badly."

"Me too," she breathed, and gasped as he leaned down and took her nipple into his mouth. His tongue ran in circles, sending thrills through her again. She'd thought once would be enough to get him out of her system, but as she felt him harden again inside her, she knew that wasn't the case.

She closed her eyes and gave herself over to him completely, all thoughts of her abandoned friend forgotten.

12
BLACK CABS & CASTING SOFAS

Pandora stretched like a cat beneath her duvet. She thought back to last night, and a smile curled the corners of her mouth. Clay had wanted her to go home with him, but she had an audition today and needed her beauty sleep. She wouldn't get the job if she turned up hungover and tired, and besides she'd promised Bea they wouldn't stay long, so ditching her friend was out of the question.

She'd expected Bea to be cross with her for disappearing. After all, Pandora had promised she wouldn't abandon her friend and had then gone on to do just that, even if it was only for an hour. But what an hour it was.

Surprisingly Bea seemed genuinely pleased for her; she even looked like she'd had a good time herself. On a high, and slightly tipsy in the cab on the way home, Bea had insisted on hearing everything that had happened and was open-mouthed to hear they'd had sex right there in the club.

"Well, it wasn't like we did it on the dance floor in front of an audience," Pandora laughed, seeing the shocked face of her straight-laced friend. The two of them were so different, but she suspected Bea had enjoyed her walk on the wild side.

Pandora wriggled under the duvet and closed her eyes as she recalled the feel of Clay's hands on her body, the thrill of giving herself over to him. She'd been adamant she would just return his jacket and see whether there was still a spark of attraction there. And boy was there still a spark.

He'd eventually and reluctantly let her go once she'd promised to go out with him later in the week.

Her eyes snapped open, and she mentally shook herself. She didn't have time to sit around mooning today. She had an audition. She needed to get up, get her game face on and get herself over to the West End. It was no good turning up in pyjamas with a just-fucked expression on her face; she had a career to build.

Alarm bells should have gone off in Pandora's brain when she discovered the audition was taking place in a hotel, but her agent had dismissed it.

"Oh honey, that's just what these American producers do. They fly over for a day or so, put up in a penthouse somewhere, do their auditioning and then fly back to Hollywood. You should be glad; otherwise, you'd have to find the money to fly over to the States to meet this guy. Larry Crowder's a big deal over there, and he wants to meet you. You put on your best face, work that famous Pandora charm and, whatever you do, don't piss him off."

Angie Beeton was a hardened talent agent, who'd been in the business for enough years to have seen and heard pretty much everything. She was tough, unshockable and didn't mince her words.

Pandora had to admit to being excited. Crowder had asked to meet her after seeing some promo footage from the gangster movie, so he must have been impressed.

After spending a couple of hours getting ready, perfecting her hair and makeup and squeezing into a fitted dress which clung to her curves, she was ready to go. Sure she could act, but there was no harm looking like a star too. She treated herself to a cab over to the hotel and was asked to wait in the bar.

She glanced wistfully over at the bottles behind the bar. She would have loved a glass of wine to calm her nerves, but she had to be professional. So instead she sat, poised, sipping a glass of water and waiting for him to arrive.

After twenty minutes or so a middle-aged woman with teased hair and a mauve trouser suit strode into the bar.

"Pandora Caine?" she drawled loudly. Pandora stood. "He's ready for you sweetie."

Pandora followed her up in the lift, trying to find some kind of small talk.

"Has Mr Crowder auditioned many people for this part?"

"Oh, he's constantly seeing people, but you're his first today," she said drily as the lift doors opened and they stepped out into the corridor. The woman slipped a keycard into the slot and held the door open. "In you go, sugar."

Pandora hesitated. "You're not coming in?"

"No. You're a big girl, off you go. He won't bite," she chuckled, "unless you want him to."

Pandora took a breath and pulled her shoulders back. There was no point creeping in looking timid; after all, he'd asked to see her. *Come on,* she urged herself, *act the star you want to be.* She put a megawatt smile on her face and walked into the room.

She'd expected to walk in and be greeted by him but was surprised to find the room empty. *Strange. Where was he?* Pandora frowned, then scolded herself. She'd get wrinkles. The door clicked shut behind her, making her jump in the silent apartment.

"Mr Crowder?" she called out.

"In here."

She followed the sound of his voice over to a different room, and put her head tentatively around the door, to discover, to her horror, that it was the bathroom and he was lying in the bath. She gasped and bolted straight back out.

She closed her eyes in horror. *Shit! She'd done it now.* He'd never give her a job after this. Could this be any more embarrassing?

She heard him chortle from the other side of the door. "Don't be shy, Pandora. We're all artists, aren't we? There's no room for prudes in this game. Come hand me a towel."

Pandora hesitated. She had two options. She could run for the hills and burn her bridges with one of the most influential producers in Hollywood, or she could brazen it out. And after all, she'd already seen everything when she'd first walked in. If anything, it was he who should be embarrassed. And if he wasn't, why the hell should she be? He was the one lounging in the bath when he should be running an audition.

She lifted her chin and walked back in, meeting his eyes and refusing to look down at his fleshy naked body or his button mushroom of a cock.

She reached for a towel and held it out to him, averting her gaze with a look of disdain as he heaved himself out of the water like an emerging hippo and dried himself. Very thoroughly and without any sense of embarrassment at all. *Jeez, did this pass as normal in Hollywood?* She stepped back outside and waited for him to emerge. When he did, the towel was tied around his waist. *Thank goodness for that.*

Maybe he was some kind of nudist. Maybe this was normal behaviour in Hollywood. She followed him through to the living room where he sat himself down on the sofa, legs splayed apart, which didn't do much to hide his modesty in the towel. His comment about her being a prude had stung, so she tried to ignore his weird attire. She didn't want to offend him.

"So, I saw the rushes from your recent movie, and I liked what I saw. I could do great things with a girl like you in Hollywood."

"Really?" she breathed, all embarrassment forgotten. This could be her big break.

"Now, I know you can act, I've seen that on screen. But tell me, did you use a body double in the movie?"

She laughed indignantly. "No, of course not! They're definitely all my own assets."

"Show me."

Pandora paused, not sure she'd understood correctly. "What?"

"You heard me. Show me it wasn't just movie magic and makeup. If I'm going to catapult you to stardom, I need to know you're the real deal."

Pandora paused. This was odd, and not what she'd expected at all. But she supposed he had a point. Besides she'd already posed for a nearly naked calendar, so she had to stop being so hesitant about showing off her body.

"Come on. I'm a busy man. I don't have all day."

She stood, and holding her arms out to the sides gave him a 360-degree turn.

He shook his head. "A dress can hide a multitude of sins; we all know that."

Pandora sighed; that was true. She closed her eyes for a second then unzipped her dress and wriggled it down. Thank goodness she'd put decent underwear on today. She stood, feeling slightly foolish as he looked her up and down.

Crowder nodded approvingly. "Come here," he said, beckoning with a podgy finger.

She walked towards him until she was standing inches away from his knees.

"Turn around.'

Pandora wished she'd worn less sexy underwear or at least something that gave her a little more coverage. But thinking dreamily of Clay as she'd dressed, she'd picked out a lacy black thong and matching bra. It was fuck-me underwear. She would have loved to wear it for Clay, but it left her feeling very exposed right now, especially as this guy was so bloody close to her.

She glanced over her shoulder and gasped as she saw Larry's towel had come undone, and he had his cock in his hand. He smirked, his eyes never leaving her arse.

"You're certainly the real deal, darlin'. I could give you a big career."

Pandora tried to ignore his moving hand and concentrate on what he was saying. He continued, his voice low and breathy. "You have what it takes to be a big star, and I can make that happen for you." He raised his eyes to hers, challenging. "As they say, you scratch my back; I'll scratch yours.

Pandora stood, frozen.

Larry took his hand away. "Now how about you show me how well we could work together?" He smiled, and his cock twitched.

Pandora backed away, humiliation giving way to anger. "Are you fucking kidding me? Suck my cock, and I'll make you a star? That's what you're offering?"

"You said it. After all, I can make you famous."

Pandora picked up her dress off the sofa and started wriggling furiously back into it, her face crimson.

"No way! I wouldn't touch that with a ten-foot pole. I'd never be that desperate."

Larry tutted mockingly. "Wrong decision darlin'. Are you sure you want to make an enemy of me for the sake of five minutes of your time? Don't forget, I can make you, but I can also make sure you never work in this industry again."

Pandora turned back to him, eyes flashing. "Fuck you, you fat little pervert."

And she stormed out of the room to the sound of his laughter.

Once the lift doors slid shut, Pandora covered her face with her hands and sank to a crouch. She was shaking; she wasn't sure whether it was anger, shock or adrenaline. *What the hell had just happened?*

She'd thought she was going for a job interview and she'd ended up being treated like a two-bit whore. As the lift pinged, she rose unsteadily to her feet, her head reeling. The doors opened to the reception area, and she spotted Crowder's PA sitting on one of the sofas and stormed over.

"Did you know that was going to happen?" she demanded.

The woman shrugged in a world-weary way.

"Sweetie, I never know what's going to happen from one moment to the next. I just roll with the punches."

"Why do you work for a creep like that? You could at least have warned me!"

The woman gave her a flat stare.

"Sugar, once you've been in this business for as long as I have nothing surprises you. You might have turned him down, but he's auditioning another two girls today, and there's a good chance at least one of them will be keener to get ahead than you were."

"What?"

"Oh bless your heart, ain't you a fresh one?" she cackled.

Pandora huffed and marched furiously out onto the street. *These people were all mad!*

Needing a rant, Pandora headed straight over to her agent's office. She couldn't face going straight home. *How would Angie react? She couldn't have known Crowder would pull a stunt like that, surely. Would she be shocked by it?* No matter how industry-hardened Angie was, surely she wouldn't have knowingly sent her into that situation? Not without warning at least!

Words echoed around Pandora's head as the cab crawled its way through the London traffic.

"Don't piss him off."

"You'll never work again."

"Isn't it worth five minutes of your time?"

Her lips pressed together as anger coursed through her.

But when she arrived at the office, Pandora was disappointed. Angie's bored assistant informed her she was out for the afternoon and refused to tell Pandora where she was. *Probably some boozy lunch somewhere, the woman had a liver tougher than boot leather.* Deflated, but not prepared to give any details to the officious cow behind the desk, Pandora left a message asking for an urgent callback.

The London traffic was heavy and slow, and no matter how much she wanted to Pandora really couldn't afford another taxi. So, turning a blind eye to the stares of the other passengers she got on a bus, gazing fixedly out of an upstairs window. That was one blessing about living in London. You were more likely to win the lottery than you were to have someone talk to you on public transport, and being lost amongst strangers for the hour-long journey was a welcome relief.

It was nearly five when Pandora finally got home to an empty flat. She kicked off her heels and poured herself a large glass of wine, drinking it far faster than she planned to, then marched into her bedroom and angrily shucked the dress, pulling on trackie bottoms and a sweatshirt and scrubbing off her makeup. She wanted to get rid of every reminder of the horrible day. Then she took the bottle and curled up in the corner of the sofa. She hadn't eaten all day, so the wine took immediate effect, making her feel woozy and numb. But it didn't still the voices echoing around in her head.

Was that really what you needed to do to get ahead? She thought of her Hollywood idols and wondered what they'd done to land their first big role. She shuddered as an image of Larry swam into her head again and she slopped more wine into her glass.

The phone rang. She didn't want to talk to anyone right now but glanced at the screen all the same. It was her agent.

"Hi, Angie."

"I'm guessing the audition didn't go so well?"

How did she know that?

"I've just had Larry Crowder on the phone. He was rather scathing about your acting ability and suggested I drop you from my books."

Pandora's mouth gaped. "You've got to be kidding me?" She glanced over to the door as Bea let herself into the flat, giving her a little wave. Pandora felt a pang of resentment. Bea's life was so much more straightforward than hers. She went into her bedroom and shut the door; she didn't need Bea hearing this; it was humiliating enough telling Angie. "That bastard! He wanted me to blow him to get the part!"

Angie chuckled.

"It's not funny!"

"I know it isn't honey, and it's not like he's the most attractive man in the world is he?" She paused, and Pandora heard her take a drag on a cigarette. "So tell me what happened."

"I was standing there in my underwear, and when I turned around, he had his cock in his hand and said I'd never work again if I didn't suck him off!"

There was a pause on the other end of the line which to Pandora sounded slightly judgmental.

"I have to ask. Why were you in your underwear?"

Pandora sighed, feeling foolish. "He gave me some bullshit line about proving I didn't use a body double." It sounded so stupid now she said it to someone else. She could almost see Angie shaking her head on the other end of the phone.

"Oh honey, how can you look the way you do and still

be so naïve? Well, good for you for storming out and taking the moral high-ground. But I have to be honest, Larry Crowder blacklisting you is going to make things a lot tougher. I'd put any ideas of Hollywood on the back burner for now and concentrate on getting work locally." She paused. "There's something else that you're not going to want to hear, but it's probably best you hear it from me."

Pandora's heart sank. *What now? Surely the day couldn't get any worse?*

"Larry's given the part to Rhiannon Reeves."

"Seriously? But she's just some bit part soap actress! She can't even act! I can't believe she got down on her knees to land the role."

"Either way I thought you should know. Listen, you get some rest, and we'll regroup tomorrow."

Pandora threw the phone down and drained her glass. What she needed was a long soak in the bath to try and wash the day away.

Pandora sank below the surface of the water, relishing the heat and comfort of the bath. Resurfacing with a gasp, she heard Bea shout that she was going out and would see her later. *That was unusual, Bea hardly ever went out, she was a total homebody. Perhaps she was doing an evening class or something.*

But it was no bad thing. Pandora didn't feel like company tonight.

She lay there, eyes closed, her body relaxing in the scented water when she felt a draft and heard the door slam. *Bea must have forgotten something.*

A moment later, she felt a finger brush her cheek, and her eyes flew open. Startled, she sat up sloshing water all over the floor. Clay grinned down at her.

"Sorry, I didn't mean to scare you."

Pandora, adrenaline coursing through her system, wasn't sure whether to hit him or pull him into the bath with her. She sat there, hands covering her chest, her heart racing as she recovered from the shock.

"Your flatmate let me in", he grimaced apologetically and looked relieved when she laughed.

"Christ, you scared the life out of me! Chuck me a towel, will you?"

What a day, and to top it all off Clay was now seeing her with no makeup, and literally stripped bare. So much for the illusion of her being a glamorous movie star. She'd desperately wanted to retain some of the mystery; she couldn't help feeling he'd rapidly tire of her if he thought she was just some ordinary girl.

Oh well, he was here now. There was no point telling him to wait outside while she dolled herself up for him.

He held out a fluffy white dressing gown, and she wrapped it around her shoulders. She twisted her wet hair in a towel.

"Ta-dah!" she laughed arms stretched wide. "How glamorous do I look now?"

He took her in his arms and murmured, "You look sensational."

She snorted, "I bet I do!"

But he stilled her with a kiss which deepened and became more urgent. Pandora melted into him. This was precisely what she needed. He was the perfect tonic to a crappy day.

Later they lay entwined in Pandora's bed, sated and happy, her head on his chest and leg thrown possessively across him. This was a good moment; she wanted to hold onto it.

But Clay, it seemed, had other ideas.

"So, how did your audition go?"

Pandora's blissful mood evaporated. Even in the afterglow of sex, the thought of Larry Crowder pulled her up sharp.

"Not great," she mumbled.

"How come?" Clay stroked her hair, smiling at the wild, bouncy curls that had formed from her hair drying naturally.

"I don't want to talk about it." She sat up and grabbed her dressing gown. "I'm going to get a drink, want one?"

"Sure."

Clay lay there for a minute, frowning. *Well, that had been a total mood change. What the hell had happened today?*

Pulling on his boxers, he jogged after her. She opened a fresh bottle of wine and poured them both a glass, handing him one. He waited. The silence between them stretched.

"So, are you going to tell me what happened?"

"Nothing important, just some creep."

"And what did this creep do?"

Pandora shrugged and for a moment looked like a petulant teenager. She took a sip of wine. "It doesn't matter. How come you're here, anyway? I thought you were working tonight?"

"I snuck out." He folded his arms. "Now tell me."

She sighed and padded through to the living room, tucking her legs underneath her on the sofa. Clay chose the armchair facing her and sat, waiting for her to speak. He wasn't going to let her shrug this off.

Reluctantly Pandora told him the whole story, and to her dismay found herself in tears. She felt such a bloody fool. She'd been duped into taking her clothes off as well as messing up any chance of a Hollywood career. She'd probably blown things with Clay too. He'd run a mile after tonight. He must have wondered what the hell had happened to his glamorous starlet. She'd transformed into a snivelling wretch, like Cinderella in reverse. Talk about shattering the illusion. The thought made her tears come even faster.

Clay didn't move as she told her story. He let her sob and rant and get it out of her system. When she'd finished, he pulled her into his arms and held her tight.

"Nobody will ever treat you like that again, you understand?"

She leaned into him, savouring the comfort of his

embrace. Clay held her, his face like stone. That fucker wouldn't get away with this; it didn't matter how important he thought he was.

Clay would make him pay.

13
GREASY CHIPS & CONFIDENCES

The motley crew of stragglers in the fish and chip shop cleared out as soon as Frankie entered. If he was here, he wanted privacy. The Codfather, as Frankie had wittily named it, was his unofficial office. It did a quiet trade made up almost entirely of Frankies' employees. Anyone else who wandered in off the street was given stale cold chips to discourage them from returning. Frankies' boys, on the other hand, got everything freshly cooked out back.

Nodding respectfully, they wished Frankie a good evening and closed the door behind them, turning the sign to closed.

Chris watched them leave in surprise.

"Something I said?"

Frankie chuckled, and they sat down at one of the Formica tables, which seemed ridiculously small for two such large men. They'd just left the gym after another bout. This time Frankie had called ahead to arrange to spar with Chris. It made a nice change to have someone give him a proper fight in the ring. Everyone else was either too crap or too scared to really give it some.

Chris was a quiet kid but tough. Frankie respected that. He was surrounded by people who were all mouth and no trousers, running their mouths off the whole time. That made Chris a refreshing change.

"Don't worry; I own this place."

"How come it's so quiet on a Saturday night?"

"We work hard to keep it that way. I don't make my money selling greasy chips, and cash businesses are always useful if you catch my drift."

A woman with a smoker's face, wearing a short denim skirt and high wedge shoes, appeared at the table.

"Y'alright, Frankie? What can I get for you boys?" She looked Chris up and down with appraising eyes. "I say, who's this tall drink of water you've brought in? And here I am feelin' thirsty an' all." She cackled and fanned herself theatrically.

"Leave it out, Crystal. We didn't come here for the company. Two haddock and chips and two cups of tea. Now fuck off."

He shook his head as Crystal tottered back off to the kitchen.

When Crystal returned she was wearing a newly applied coat of hot pink lipstick, and Frankie detected an unwelcome waft of hairspray and cheap perfume over the smell of the food.

Frankie liberally splashed vinegar and the salt on his chips and took a mouthful. He was starving.

"Now Chris," he said, mid-chew, "tell me a bit about yourself."

So while Frankie ate, Chris told him about his job working in a warehouse, how it was long hours and low pay, but he didn't have much choice as he'd had to drop out of school before he could do his exams. He'd been working there for three years now, living at home with his mum who wasn't well. When he wasn't working, he looked after her.

"What about your dad?"

Chris shrugged. "It's always just been mum and me."

Frankie watched the boy greedily tuck into his dinner. He looked tired. He clearly had a lot on his plate, and Frankie wondered whether the mum was a lot poorlier than he was letting on. Frankie respected that the kid was working hard to look after his family, that was good. But someone his age should be able to go out and have fun from time to time, not have to carry the weight of the world on his shoulders.

"Sounds tough," said Frankie. "But I respect what you're doing. It takes a big man to take on a responsibility like that at your age. How old are you? Seventeen?"

"Eighteen," Chris mumbled, mouth full of batter.

Just then, the door swung open, and a dark-haired man in a hoodie ambled in. Frankie stilled, watching him with narrowed eyes, so Chris - his curiosity piqued – turned and watched him too.

"Chips please doll," he said in an Eastern European accent with the hint of a cockney twang.

Crystal looked bored and shovelled some cool soggy chips into a bag.

She pushed them over the counter.

"Ain't you got nothing fresher? These look like they were cooked last week."

Crystal shrugged.

The room was silent except for the tinny sound of a radio playing pop music in the back. Chris looked on, wondering whether there was about to be trouble. But after a tense moment, the guy took his cold chips, threw a few coins on the counter, and walked back out onto the street. Frankie's eyes followed him until the door swung shut behind him.

"Who was that?"

Frankie rubbed his jaw. "Judging by his accent, I'd say he's one of the Albanians. They've been gradually moving in around here, and it's beginning to wind me up."

Chris waited patiently for Frankie to elaborate.

"It's not like they've done anything to step on my toes. Not that I know of anyway. If anything they've been careful not to. They run knocking shops and massage parlours, which they know I'm not into. Linda's a possessive woman. It's never been worth the aggro."

"So, what's the problem?"

Frankie forked the last mouthful of chips into his mouth and chewed as he mulled this over. "The way I see it, if the Albanians are running a seedy sex racket, there's a good chance they're also people smuggling. And if they're bringing people into the country illegally what else are they importing? That's where I can see it starting to affect my business, and I can't have that."

"You think him coming in here was some kind of message?"

"Either that or he was casing the joint. Or he could just be some random idiot who doesn't know any better. I'm hearing Albanian accents wherever I go at the moment. Don't know if I'm paranoid or if we've got ourselves an infestation."

"People pay you protection though, right? Are they paying?"

"No, we've left them alone so far. Getting involved will only tie us into their dodgy dealings. It's the police they need protecting from, and I'm not inclined to help them with that. If they get busted and sent back home, that's my problem sorted."

"Is it worth having a word with a friendly policeman? I'm guessing you know a few. Stir things up a bit for them."

"I certainly do. You know that's not a bad idea." Frankie smiled as a plan started to form. Chris glanced at his watch. "I'd better be getting back Mr Finch; mum will be wondering where I am."

"Of course. Why not take some fish and chips back for her too? Oy, Crystal!"

Crystal glanced up; she'd been leaning on the counter reading a magazine, her lips moving slightly as she deciphered the text.

"Bag up another haddock and chips to take away, will you? And make it sharpish."

Frankie turned back to Chris. "Give your mum a bit of a treat. Everyone likes fish and chips, don't they?"

"Thanks, Mr Finch, she'll love that."

"You know, that reminds me, I don't even know your surname. What is it?"

"Slaughter. Chris Slaughter."

Frankie barked a laugh. "Really? Slaughter indeed. I like that. I like that a lot."

14
BITCHES & BONFIRES

Ivy was worried about Clay. She was used to his womanising. It almost didn't bother her any more, but this was different. For the first time, he was smitten by someone, and it was affecting his judgement.

Despite Frankie's warning, Clay was letting things slip. At work, he wasn't concentrating, let alone thinking of new ways to promote the club. He'd also been bunking off to see Pandora, leaving Ivy in the uncomfortable position of having to cover for him. He'd apologised the first time, promising it was a one-off, but now he didn't even ask any more, he just assumed she'd cover him if he didn't show. It was sheer dumb luck that Frankie hadn't come in on a night when Clay was absent.

Also, there was the incident a few nights ago when he turned up at her house late one night in bloodstained clothes, looking wired. He'd thrown gravel at her bedroom window to wake her, nearly cracking the glass. She didn't know what time it was, but it wasn't quite dawn yet as she peered down into the dark street. "I need your help," he hissed.

She crept downstairs trying not to wake her mum and opened the door.

"Thanks, Ivy, you're a gem. I didn't know where else to go," he whispered as she shushed him inside.

She didn't ask what had happened. She didn't want to know. But as he emerged from the shower, a towel around his waist, she looked him over and noted that there wasn't a scratch on him. So wherever the blood had come from it had belonged to someone else, and it couldn't have been a fight. Clay was handy with his fists but not so handy to get away without a few bruises himself. Had Frankie got him doing something else on the side? She didn't think Clay was involved with anything like that, but then if Frankie gave him a job what choice would he have had?

Her brother was in the army, and off on tour; otherwise, Clay might have had a harder time of it. As it was, he borrowed a pair of Jack's jeans and a t-shirt, and she'd burned the bloody clothes in the garden incinerator. Standing in the cold dawn air, she watched the flames crackle, and the smoke rise until the pink glow on the horizon was almost daylight. Then she went back to bed.

The whole incident bothered her, but she'd barely seen Clay since to ask him about it.

Frankie was due in the club tonight, so Clay had better show. Ivy might be annoyed with the way he was behaving, but she didn't want him to get fired.

Looking on the bright side at least he'd dropped his usual nightly seduction routine. Watching an endless procession of women line up to lose their knickers in his office wasn't her idea of a good time. She just wasn't sure this obsession with Pandora was an improvement.

At least with Frankie in things would go back to normal. No Casanova act, no Pandora, no skiving, just an uneventful evening.

That reminded her, she needed to cheer up and put a brave face on things for work tonight. She had to admit to being in a bad mood lately, not helped by nagging anxiety because she'd missed her period. It was unlikely that she was pregnant, but she was starting to wonder whether that was a possibility.

They'd only skipped protection one time. And what were the odds of her getting pregnant from one random night? At least that's what she told herself until her period didn't arrive.

Of course, this was all made worse by Pandora being on the scene.

In the back of her mind, Ivy had always thought Clay would stand by her if she fell pregnant, that he just needed a good reason to leave his alley-cat ways behind him and settle down. But now she wasn't sure. He'd changed over the last few weeks. He seemed to be drifting further and further away from the boy she'd known and loved for years.

Still, he would come to his senses soon enough. Ivy had never seen him stay keen on anyone after the initial thrill of the chase was over. She was the only girl he always came back to.

But the worry was starting to affect her sleep, and when she looked at herself in the bathroom mirror, she looked drawn and dowdy. The late nights were putting years on her. She'd turn into her mum soon, all she needed was a housecoat and some curlers. Was it any wonder Clay was with Pandora instead of her?

On a whim, she grabbed her handbag and set off down to the hairdressers on the high street.

The hairdresser was a cute guy with an implausibly tall quiff. *You can tell he gets a discount on hair products,* she thought dryly to herself. He was only too happy to give her a total hair makeover.

Ivy sat in the chair as they fastened a gown around her shoulders and looked at herself in the mirror. In his sweeter moments, Clay said she looked like Rita Hayworth with her mane of auburn hair, but right now the girl looking back at her looked just plain ordinary. It was time for that to change.

By the time she walked into the club that night, feeling a little self-conscious, Ivy looked a different woman. Clementine immediately did a double-take and greeted her with a rapturous welcome. "Hey look at you girl! You look like something brand shiny and new!"

Ivy wanted the floor to swallow her up as the rest of the staff gathered around, telling her how great she looked, but while the attention made her uncomfortable, she felt a glow of pleasure. She'd felt fearless at the hairdressers, but since wondered if she'd made a huge mistake. The compliments were definitely helping though.

Clay came over to see what the commotion was and raised an eyebrow.

"What have you done to yourself, Ivy?"

Clementine shoved him. "What the hell kind of thing is that to say to a woman who's just come out of the hairdressers?"

"Sorry," he grimaced. "You look great Ivy. You just, well..." he struggled for the right words, "you just don't look like you."

She turned and went to hang her coat up, fighting back hot tears. She didn't want to admit even to herself that she'd done this in the hope that he would like it, but it stung for him to be so dismissive. *Why couldn't he just be nice?*

Clementine put an arm around her shoulders.

"You're not letting that idiot get to you again, are you? You need to find yourself a boy who's going to treat you right. Not some idiot gangster lothario who can't see the bundle of gorgeousness that's right in front of him."

"Thanks, Clem," she mumbled and took a deep breath. Clementine used a tissue to dab her friend's eyes and repair the smeared makeup, then stood back and looked at her. She nodded approvingly. "Good as new. Come on, time to get out there and slap that smile on your face."

Ivy pulled her shoulders back and headed over to the bar.

Sod Clay. She had work to do.

Ivy was surprised by how much more male attention she got that evening. Could going blonde really make that much of a difference? Almost every man who came to the bar seemed to be chatting her up. Or perhaps they just sensed her change in attitude. She was feeling defiant, that she didn't give a damn, and maybe that showed.

Frankie arrived at nine and, true to form was perfectly charming about her new look. According to him, she looked even more beautiful than usual, and he was sure bar takings would be up tonight just because of it.

He was very sweet although Ivy wondered whether Clementine had put him up to it. Either way, she started to feel better.

Sadly that wouldn't last.

Before long there was a general stir in the crowd, and when Ivy looked over to see what was causing it, her heart sank.

Pandora was wearing yet another photograph-inducing outfit and looked sensational. Ivy idly wondered how long it took her to get ready; it must take bloody ages. Or perhaps, she thought despairingly, she just woke up like that.

She watched as Pandora wiggled her fingers at Clay who flashed her a big grin and mouthed "be right there."

Pandora walked over to the bar. Her body swaying, she took every man's eyes with her. Sliding onto a bar stool, the guy next to her immediately offered her a drink. Ivy rolled her eyes. *What was wrong with everyone? She was like a fucking disease.*

"Glass of champagne please," she purred with a slow smile.

Of course, she would order champagne, thought Ivy, who'd never been bought champagne in her life. She was lucky if she got bought half a lager and a packet of crisps.

She slid the drinks across the bar, and Pandora's eyes focused on her, widening in surprise.

"Oh wow," she exclaimed in exaggerated astonishment. "Look at you! You've gone blonde! Well, blondes do have more fun," she laughed, then leaned forward conspiratorially so nobody else could hear. "Between you and me, it's always best to get your hair dyed in a salon if you can afford it darling, you can always tell when someone's done a cheap home dye job."

Ivy's eyes narrowed. "It was done at a hairdresser actually."

Pandora's mouth stretched into a nasty smile. "Oh dear, really? Perhaps it's just you that makes it look cheap then."

Ivy gaped. *What a bitch!*

Just then Clay came over and slid his arms around Pandora, kissing her neck. She leaned into him, smiling, her triumphant eyes on Ivy's.

"Come on, babe, come and meet Frankie. Send over a bottle of champagne, will you Ivy?"

Frankie was enjoying himself, his usual anxiety had faded, at least for a while, and he was rather taken with Pandora. He could see why Clay liked her; after all, her assets were rather obvious, but maybe that was needed to keep him interested and stop his constant prowling for new conquests.

Clay was on top form, keeping the conversation flowing and the mood high, and Frankie found to his surprise that he was having fun. Perhaps the club was getting some of its sparkle back. Or perhaps he was. This was why he employed Clay, and it was good to see him on form. Maybe he'd been a bit harsh before. Or maybe that kick up the arse had done the trick.

He tuned back into Pandora who was telling them about a disastrous school musical she'd once starred in. A power cut after the opening scene meant they'd had to plough through the whole of *Annie* in a gradually darkening room without any musical accompaniment. "As if it wasn't humiliating enough wearing that ginger wig to start with! Can you imagine?" She laughed, as Ivy banged a tray of drinks down on the table.

Ouch, those two clearly didn't get on. Frankie wasn't surprised. He couldn't imagine many women wanting to be best friends with an apex predator like Pandora, and Ivy had always held a candle for Clay. He dismissed the thought, after all, it wasn't his problem. And besides, the glimmer of a brilliant idea was forming.

"So you can sing then?"

"Is the pope Catholic Frankie?"

"I mean properly sing, not just hold a tune?"

"Of course. Why? What did you have in mind?"

"How about doing a set for us next Saturday night?"

Pandora's eyes gleamed. She loved performing live. That was the one disappointment about making movies; it was cold and clinical with just the reaction of the Director to go on. In her mind's eye, she could already hear the applause and feel the adoration of the audience.

"I'll have to check my schedule of course, but how could I say no to you, Frankie? I'd love to!"

15
SCRAPING THE BARREL

"Look, darling," drawled Angie, "I'm just saying you could do with some publicity to get things moving. You're sliding into obscurity, and after that incident with Larry, God rest his soul, and the son of a bitch bad-mouthing you all over town the phone's hardly been ringing off the hook."

Pandora huffed. Bloody Crowder. She wished she'd never gone to that audition.

"What do you mean 'God rest his soul?'"

"Oh, you didn't hear? I forgot you've been in your loved-up bubble for the last few weeks. You must be very keen on this new boyfriend of yours! Larry's dead, honey. Murdered in his hotel suite!"

"Seriously?"

"Of course seriously. Even I'm not going to joke about that, no matter what an arse the man was."

"Oh," said Pandora, taken aback. Then, as the memory of her experience in his hotel room flooded back, she added, "It couldn't have happened to a nicer man."

"Well, totally. And actually, this is good news for you.

Unless you killed him of course," she cackled. "Crowder might have spread some poison about you after you knocked him back, but that'll pass now that he has. We just need to get you back onto the public's radar, get some coverage in the papers, maybe a few interviews. I have to be honest with you; things are running a little dry at this end, and I'm not talking about my menopause."

She paused for a minute, dragging on her ever-present cigarette. "Can't you start an affair with someone famous? Or get married or something, darling? We desperately need to get you some column inches."

"Frankie Finch offered me a spot singing at The Flamingo Club on Saturday night. Maybe we could get some coverage from that?"

"A one-off gig in an East End club is all well and good but let's be honest; it's hardly going to catapult you to international stardom is it?"

Pandora sighed.

"Oh Angie, I knew this wasn't going to be easy, but I did think it would be less about publicity and more about actual acting."

"You are sweet. Of course, that's how it works, once you're famous. The problem is you have to get famous before they even look at your acting. All I can say is: you do you, honey. I'm sure some casting director will hire you for your ability and not your more obvious talents." Angie took another drag on her cigarette and exhaled a stream of smoke. "On a brighter note, I have had a job offer for you. It's not what you were hoping for, but it's work, and it'll pay the bills, including mine, don't forget. Remember the audition you did with that theatre company? They want you to be Jack in *Jack and the Beanstalk* down in Brighton."

Pandora groaned.

"Well, I'm not sure you can afford to be like that about it," Angie reprimanded. "If you're too picky you won't be working at all. Besides, it's two months of solid work, and if they like you, you might get a longer contract. Maybe working in a rep would be good for you. Keep your head down until the whole Larry Crowder thing has blown over. Plus it's all experience. Better to keep working than have gaps on your CV while you pull pints to make ends meet."

Pandora thought of Ivy. There was no way she was doing bar work. "I suppose you're right."

Besides, she shouldn't be disappointed, there were plenty of actors out there who'd be glad for the panto job, but it was hardly A list stuff. She'd just done a major movie, no matter how minor the role had been, and she had a taste for it. She'd have to rack her brains for a way to get back in the papers.

"What about a reality show or something?"

"I can put some feelers out for you, but my advice would be to take this job and be grateful for it."

Ending the call, Pandora flipped the switch on the kettle, trying to think of some publicity ideas while she waited for the water to boil. A few months ago, her star had been on the rise, and everything had looked so promising. Was she really on a downward slide already? All because she'd refused to suck some guy's cock?

At drama school, they'd joked that panto was where actors went to die, like the acting community's retirement home. But that was with the naïve confidence of students, and before any of them had actually been out of work.

Besides if she didn't work, she'd run out of money and have to move back in with her parents, and there was no way she was doing that. The only job she'd got recently was an ad campaign for a new perfume, that was hardly going to win her a Golden Globe. But then working in a panto certainly beat getting a bar job to pay the bills.

Her mum and dad had always been dead-set against her being an actress, which they saw as a slightly grubby profession. In their comfortable, middle-class house in the suburbs, they thought actresses were only one step up from prostitutes. *Why couldn't she marry a nice doctor or get a job in PR like her cousin Susan?*

Pandora had sworn to make it big and prove them wrong, but it looked like her journey wasn't going to be a smooth one. And then there was Clay. Her heart lurched as she thought about breaking the news to him that she'd be moving down to Brighton.

16
RAZZLE DAZZLE & DIAMONDS

Clay drummed his fingers against the wall. He wasn't one to get nervous, but he had proper butterflies tonight. Pandora was getting ready for her performance, and she'd shooed him out, claiming his office as a dressing room.

He was still reeling after she told him about the panto job yesterday. How could she think of moving to Brighton? They were having such a great time, seeing each other every night, hardly able to keep their hands off each other. Clay wasn't one for relationships, but they both seemed to have fallen into this without any hesitation. As much as it bothered him to admit it, the thought of her moving away had totally thrown him.

But after giving it some thought he'd hatched a plan. It was a risky one, but it might just work.

The club was buzzing even more than a typical Saturday night; he could hear the thrum of excitement. Frankie had handpicked their best clients and invited them, and the atmosphere was electric. Clay had almost forgotten how the club felt back in its heyday when it first opened, but it was like this. And that was all thanks to Pandora.

As if on cue, the office door opened and Clay's jaw dropped. Pandora looked amazing. She always looked amazing, but tonight she was nothing short of breathtaking. On first glance, she looked naked except for some strategically scattered diamonds, but as he looked closer, he saw she was wearing a flesh-coloured mesh dress with thousands of crystals sprinkled all over it, clustering over the hips and breasts and down the skirt but leaving the rest of her body exposed. Clay's first reaction was *wow*. His second was to tell her to get back in there and put some clothes on. He might get to see her looking like this, but he wasn't sure he wanted the rest of the club to.

She paused, eyeing his reaction, sudden doubt on her face. "Don't you like it? Is it too much?"

Clay chuckled. "Like it? You look incredible! I'm just not sure I want to share you with the rest of the club."

She laughed relieved. "Ah well, you have to share me with my public I'm afraid. But remember, it's only you that I'm going home with tonight."

He grinned back at her, eyes drinking her in as he ran a hand appreciatively around her waist. That was a good point. He took her hand. "Are you ready to do this then?"

She nodded, and he squeezed her hand before they headed out into the club.

On seeing them appear, Frankie got to his feet and strode up onto the stage, his presence immediately commanding the room, which fell silent.

"Good evening everyone and welcome to The Flamingo Club. As you know, tonight is a very special night, and I'd like to thank you all for coming. Without further ado, it's my pleasure to introduce to you, the fabulous Pandora Caine."

The lights dimmed, and there was a collective ripple across the room as Pandora took Frankie's hand and sashayed up the steps to the stage.

For a few moments, she stood, dress sparkling in the spotlight as the room stilled. Then, once she had everyone's attention, she closed her eyes and started to sing.

As the first smoky notes rang out, Frankie breathed a sigh of relief. He'd trusted her when she'd said she could sing. Thank goodness she'd been telling the truth. Plus that girl knew how to hold an audience.

As the band kicked in and the tempo increased Pandora swayed to the music, the crystals on her dress winking and catching the light. Like an enchantress, she'd captured every eye in the room. Frankie grinned over at Clay. "Nice one," he said.

Pandora was on stage for nearly an hour, and she did Frankie proud. At the end, she was greeted by whistling, catcalls and rapturous applause. Clay felt his heart swell with pride, but it only hardened his resolve for what he had to do next.

Pandora was elated. This night just couldn't get any better. As much as she'd loved working on the movie, there was nothing like a live audience to make you feel alive. Her face was beaming as she leaned back against Clay's desk. The skin-tight dress was fragile and unsuited to sitting down, plus she'd been lent it for tonight after Angie had called in a few favours. She needed to return it in perfect condition. The door opened, and she smiled as Clay entered carrying a bottle of champagne and two glasses.

"That," he said putting the glasses down and popping the champagne, "was amazing. You were amazing. You had that audience eating out of the palm of your hand."

She beamed, and they clinked glasses. The champagne was deliciously chill as it slid down her throat. Clay moved closer and ran a hand down the side of her dress, leaning in to kiss her. Pandora tasted the warmth of his lips and melted against him. The attraction between them was just as strong as ever. Would it always be like this?

He pulled away from her, his brow knotted.

"As much as I love this dress," he said, "how the hell

do I get into it?"

She laughed. "I am pretty well sewn in, but I think I can help you there." And she slowly undid a hidden zip and peeled herself out of the dress.

Clay stood back against the door, appreciating the view. "Mmm," he growled, turning the key in the lock as he watched. "No underwear. If I'd known that I would have found the outfit even sexier."

She grinned back at him, dress now discarded on the floor and beckoned him towards her.

He closed the gap in an instant, and ran his hands over her, relishing the feel of her warm skin as she undressed him, removing his tie, and then undoing each button on his shirt tantalisingly slowly. Eventually, she unbuckled his belt and let his trousers fall to the floor. It was time for her eyebrows to raise.

"So I wasn't the only one not wearing underwear?"

"Yeah, but I'm not wearing any cos I forgot to do any washing. Still, it has its benefits."

She slid her arms around his waist and drew him against her, their kiss deepening, everything else forgotten. Pandora wrapped her legs around him, pulling him in closer.

But Clay resisted. She opened her eyes, frowning.

"Hey," she murmured, "don't stop." And she reached to pull him back again.

"No," he said. "There's something I need to do first. And with that, he bent down, reaching for his trousers in the pile of discarded clothes on the floor. Pandora stood impatiently watching him. Finding what he was looking for he looked back up at Pandora, who was standing above him, legs gloriously parted, pouting crossly.

"What *are* you doing?"

He didn't reply, instead ran a hand up her leg, and placed a kiss on her thigh. He smiled as her head rocked back, and his kisses moved higher until she was squirming in frustration. He paused before giving her a long slow lick making her moan.

Then he stopped.

She looked at him, her face exasperated.

"What the hell are you playing at?"

He knelt just far enough away that their bodies weren't touching and held her gaze. Pandora frowned. *What was going on with him tonight?*

He pulled his hand from behind his back and held out a little velvet box, which he opened.

She gasped as she spied the huge diamond inside.

"Marry me," he said.

Pandora gaped at Clay, and then back at the ring, her eyes wide, heart hammering. She looked back at him and saw how nervous he looked before realising she'd been staring at him speechless for about a minute.

"Yes!" she said. "Of course, I'll marry you."

The relief that flooded his face was so sweet, she almost laughed, but her heart was pounding too hard. He took the ring out of the box and slid it onto her finger.

"Thank Christ for that."

"Now I know why you've been acting funny all evening!" She smiled at him; then he caught her lips with his and their desire flooded back.

"Now, where were we?"

As he sank back between her legs, Pandora sighed and stretched out her hand to admire the ring before closing her eyes and gripping the desk as waves of pleasure rolled over her.

Sometime later, flushed and giggling they emerged from the office. Pandora had changed into a more practical midnight blue dress, it was tight and strapless, and while it wasn't as risqué as her previous outfit, she could at least sit down. They went and joined Frankie at his table.

Frankie greeted Pandora like a long lost daughter, immediately clocking the diamond on her finger. There wasn't much Frankie Finch missed. He took her hand and examined it.

"Now that's new," he said. "Have you two got something to tell me?" Pandora grinned and looked back at Clay, who had an equally idiotic smile plastered across his face.

Bea, realising what had happened, jumped up and Frankie stepped out of the way as she squealed and gave her flatmate a tight squeeze. Soon the whole table was congratulating them. Frankie called for more champagne.

But Pandora caught a shadow of a frown on Bea's face when she thought no one was looking. *She thinks we're moving too fast, that I'm making a mistake.*

Even Angie looked pleased, which was a pleasant surprise until she hugged Pandora and whispered in her ear "Nice move, honey. We'll make it the showbiz wedding of the year: *the starlet and the gangste*r. It'll do wonders for your profile."

Pandora shook her head in exasperation. Angie was right though. She hadn't thought about it like that, but they could spin this brilliantly. Perhaps she wouldn't have to take that crappy job in Brighton after all.

Frankie stood and raised his glass to toast the happy couple, welcoming Pandora to the family. She beamed in response; she'd never felt happier. She couldn't wait to start shopping for a dress and planning the wedding. She could see the headlines now.

17
SICK OF IT ALL

Ivy gripped the toilet seat as she retched again. She hadn't eaten anything yet and heaved miserably on an empty stomach. As the nausea subsided, she rocked back on her heels and took a moment to catch her breath. Morning sickness had really kicked in over the past week, and it felt like she had the flu: tired, achy and constantly nauseous.

She splashed some water on her face and peered at herself in the mirror. The girl that stared back looked dreadful, pale and with dark circles under her eyes, the newly blonde hair drawing every remaining bit of colour out of her face. For the millionth time, Ivy wondered whether she should bite the bullet and just get rid of it. She couldn't afford to have a baby, and her mum would go berserk when she found out. Especially once she realised Clay was the father. She had to make a decision and fast. After all, the pregnancy couldn't stay hidden forever; she'd start showing soon.

But what was she going to do?

So far Ivy hadn't told anyone, although she was sure Clementine suspected. She wasn't against the idea of having a baby, in fact, she'd always wanted a family, but this wasn't the way she'd imagined it happening. And to make matters worse, she was finding it harder and harder to face going into work, especially after the shock of Clay and Pandora's engagement.

If she was honest, she'd been waiting for it all to go wrong between them. Clay had never been able to hold down a relationship; he'd never wanted to. He would tire of Pandora and move on as he'd always done. She never imagined for a moment that he'd marry her.

What Ivy needed was a fresh start, to get away from the club, get herself another job. She couldn't stay working with Clay; it was just too painful. Not to mention too embarrassing once he discovered she was pregnant. She would start looking for work. Hopefully, she'd find something before she had to endure their big engagement party at the end of the month.

But then, what employer would take her on if she was pregnant? Her eyes filled, and tears spilt down her cheeks. There were no two ways about it; she'd have to have a termination. She couldn't afford not to work, so it was the only practical solution.

18
FIRST CONTACT

If The Codfather was one of Frankie's offices, his greasy spoon, The Brew and Chew, was the other. Working from home wasn't ideal, not with Linda and the kids around, and neither did he want to be the bloke who stank of fish and chips the whole time, so The Brew and Chew solved that problem nicely.

It was a quiet little café, which served a cracking fry-up with strong tea, and on mornings when he didn't have a pressing engagement, Frankie would head over there for breakfast. Linda complained it would take its toll on his waistline, so he'd sometimes eat a grapefruit before he left the house to appease her. He didn't mention that he followed this with a bacon, sausage and fried-bread chaser shortly afterwards.

There were a few of his boys in the café that morning, waiting to be given jobs to do, or before they headed off to work, but other than wishing him a respectful 'Good Morning' they knew better than to bother him.

Frankie inhaled the delicious aroma as a waitress slid his plate of food in front of him. He smiled gratefully.

Nothing beats a good breakfast.

Sadly though, breakfast that day was destined to be spoilt. As he raised the first forkful to his mouth, a man burst into the café. Frankie looked him up and down: tall, skinny, nervous. He was wearing a black suit, nothing flash, but sober and respectable. Funeral even. But well worn, an everyday suit rather than one that was only pulled out on special occasions. Frankie guessed he was an undertaker.

The man's eyes darted around the room until they landed on Frankie. He nervously approached.

"Mr Finch?"

Frankie gave a sigh, his fork hovering a few inches from his mouth. Then he laid it back on the plate. So much for enjoying his breakfast in peace. He leant back and gestured to the chair in front of him—the man perched on the edge of the seat, twisting his hands. Frankie looked at him, expectantly. For fuck's sake, was he supposed to make small talk too?

After a few moments of silence, Frankie impatiently said, "Yes?" which seemed to stir the man into action.

"I need your help, Mr Finch."

Frankie waited for him to elaborate. The man bowed his head looking into his lap where his hands were clasped, his knuckles white.

"I'm in trouble."

"I guessed that. First of all, who the fuck are you?"

"Sorry, Mr Finch, my name's Sem. Sem Barker. I work up at the crematorium."

Sem from the crem, thought Frankie idly. *Catchy.*

"And exactly what kind of trouble are you in Sem?"

The man closed his eyes and took a shaky breath. Whatever his story, it was hurting him to tell it.

"I owe someone money. A lot of money. I missed a couple of payments, and now they've taken my sister."

"Who do you owe money to?"

"His name's Jorik Prifti."

"The priest," murmured Frankie.

"You know him?" asked the man, meeting Frankie's eyes for the first time. Of course, Frankie knew him; he was the Albanian mob boss.

"And why should I help you? You didn't come to me when you needed money; you went to the Albanians."

The man looked down at his hands again and shrugged miserably.

"What did you need the money for anyway?"

"I like to bet on the horses." He paused and gave a heavy sigh before continuing. "I had this sure-fire tip. I know this trainer, and he told me about this great little runner: *Golden Mile*. He was an outsider, 50:1, and he was sure to win. A win like that could have changed our lives. I put all my wages into it, then borrowed a few grand extra cos it was a sure thing. And you don't get a chance like that very often."

"So?"

"The horse fell, so I lost the money. Then because I'd blown my wages, I needed to borrow more to get through the month."

"Couldn't your boss have given you an advance?"

"My boss isn't exactly flexible, plus they don't want someone with a gambling habit working there. And besides, I'd already borrowed that couple of grand, so this was just adding a bit on top. But then they wanted the money back. They've been chasing me for weeks, turning up at the house to collect payments and the amount keeps increasing. I just don't have the kind of money they're asking for. Then I got a panicked call from mum earlier, saying they'd taken Lizzie."

The man broke down and sobbed, face in his hands.

"She's only sixteen. What the hell will they be doing with her? She must be terrified."

"Have you called the police?"

"Would you? If they had your sister?"

Frankie had to agree. But then if they'd taken his sister,

he wouldn't be sitting snivelling in some café, he would have sorted it. There would have been a fucking bloodbath.

"So, what do you want me to do?"

"Get her back. Please get her back for us."

Frankie considered. The guy was an idiot if he borrowed from the Albanians thinking there wouldn't be consequences. And why should Frankie stir up trouble for some guy he didn't know? Then again, he could use a man in the crematorium, someone who could light the fires early and occasionally burn something extra unnoticed. That could be very useful. Plus the poor mug sounded like he spent all his money in Frankie's betting shops anyway.

"Alright," he said. "I'll sort it for you. But you owe me. Understand?"

The man nodded eagerly. "Anything Frankie. I'll owe you my life. Please just get her back for me."

Frankie gave a nod. What had looked like a run of the mill day was about to get a whole lot more interesting.

Frankie assumed the massage parlour would be grim, but it exceeded his expectations. His heart sank. This was precisely why he didn't touch this business. Five pairs of eyes turned towards him as he entered. Four were girls with thin, garishly made-up faces and minimal trashy clothes. Frankie was reminded of the January sales - cheap tinsel draped around the cut-price goods to perk them up a bit.

On seeing him, the girls put on mechanical smiles and pouts, not because they liked him, but because they wouldn't eat tonight if they didn't pull in some money. And as they'd all discovered since arriving in this country, there were worse things than having to have sex with strangers.

He ignored their hopeful gazes and turned his attention to the hard-faced woman behind the counter.

"See anyone you like?" she asked in bored Slavic lilt.

"No."

"We have more girls out back," and when Frankie didn't respond, she leered, "they not young enough for you?" raising an eyebrow. "We have young girls too."

"Cut the crap. You know who I am, right?"

The woman stared levelly back at him.

"So you know you don't want to fuck with me. This girl," he said, slapping down a photo on the counter, "you took her. I want her back."

The madam gave him a slow blink and ran her tongue over her teeth, a gesture which reminded Frankie unpleasantly of a lizard. "You want a girl; you pay for her. You don't take one home."

Frankie leaned in close enough that he could smell the woman's rancid tobacco breath. "Right now, you have two options. Either you take the money the brother borrowed," he put a fat envelope down on the counter "and return the girl now. Or things go downhill fast for you. You do not want to make an enemy of me. Plus the girl's brother will have nothing left to lose, with a bit of encouragement from me there'll be police, kidnapping charges, prison sentences, and investigations of all your shitty little businesses. The police are just looking for an excuse. As am I. And what the police don't take apart, I will."

He glanced down at the envelope and gave her a wide fake smile. "Or you take your money and return the girl. Your choice."

The woman reached forward to slide the money off the counter, and Frankie slammed his hand down on top of it.

"Girl first," he growled.

The woman gave him a hate-filled stare and dialled a number, muttering furiously down the phone. She seemed to be having an argument, although maybe that was just her voice. Or perhaps Albanian was one of those languages that always sounded like people were having a row. He really needed to learn some of the lingo. *Maybe he'd get himself a Learn Albanian course for the car.*

She turned and disappeared through a beaded curtain into the back. Frankie cast his eye over the girls who were all sitting silently, their faces blank. He felt a surge of disgust. None of them had chosen this. They probably all came to Britain with the hope that the streets were paved with gold, that they could escape hardship and have a better life. Their families had probably given their entire life savings to give them the chance to come here. He shook his head. *Scumbag traffickers.*

The bead curtain was pushed aside again, and a terrified, doped girl was shoved through. Plumper than the rest, Frankie's heart lurched when he saw how young she was. But his face remained impassive. The girl was pushed towards Frankie. He lifted his hand from the envelope, and the madam snatched it and started counting. The girl stumbled, wide-eyed towards him. Frankie took her by the wrist and pulled her out onto the street.

She was silent on the drive home, which Frankie was grateful for. He didn't want to know what she'd been through. As far as he was concerned, his involvement in this sordid affair was over the minute she was safely delivered. He pulled up outside a terraced house with neat window boxes and net curtains in the windows. The door flew open, and the girl's mum ran out onto the street. She must have been watching and waiting. She probably had been for hours.

Frankie opened the passenger door for the girl, and she climbed out, looking dazed as she was enveloped in her mum's embrace. The girl stood like a statue, then appeared to realise her ordeal was over, and the two of them clasped each other sobbing.

The brother stood watching, tears brimming in his eyes. He stuck his hand out to shake Frankie's. "Thank you."

"You owe me," said Frankie ominously.

The man nodded. "Absolutely Mr Finch. Anything I can do for you, anything at all. Just let me know."

The mum unclasped the girl and said to the brother "Get her inside." Then she flung her arms around Frankie, giving him a heartfelt squeeze. Frankie stood, arms at his sides, waiting for the hug to be over.

After a few painfully long moments, she released him and planted a tear-stained kiss on his cheek.

"I'll never forget what you've done for us, Mr Finch."

Once Frankie had extricated himself from the girl's snivelling mother, he straightened his suit and climbed back in the car, relieved to escape. He hoped she hadn't got snot all over his suit.

The massage parlour incident had got him thinking. There was no doubt the Albanians were trafficking girls from Eastern Europe. And the vacant looks on their faces suggested they were being fed a regular diet of drugs to help keep them dependent on their captors. He knew none of his guys were supplying to the Albanians, which suggested they had their own supply. And that was encroaching on his business. It needed to be stamped out, and as swiftly as possible.

Frankie dialled Chris. He could do with running this past someone who didn't have an agenda. He might not have known Chris for long, but the kid had a good head on his shoulders, and Frankie trusted his gut on this one.

Besides, there was no one else he could confide in. He couldn't tell Linda, it would end up in a moral debate or an argument, and Clay was too wrapped up in his new fiancée to be of any use.

The call went to voicemail and Frankie huffed in frustration. He glanced at his watch. The kid was probably at work and wasn't allowed to have his phone on him. He'd have to wait till this evening, which sucked. The last thing he needed was to waste time in a situation like this.

Frankie wasn't used to waiting and discovered he didn't like it much. In the end, he stopped by the gym, raised a sweat to keep his frustration at bay and then got Chris's home address from Del. Instead of trying to get through on the phone, he drove over there to wait.

He sat in the car listening to the radio and smoking a cigar while he turned the problem over in his mind. Meanwhile, he kept an eye on Chris's flat. It was on the third floor of a tired-looking council block. Long concrete walkways ran past each row of front doors making each tier into its own narrow street.

It was nearly six by the time Chris appeared at his front door. For the millionth time, Frankie wondered whether he was mad putting his trust in a kid he'd only met a few weeks earlier, but all the same, it felt like the right thing to do.

After jogging up the three flights of stairs, Frankie rapped on Chris's door and waited. He glanced left and right down the walkway and noted a group of kids loitering in the far stairwell, smoking and probably looking for trouble. *Little shits, they needed to get themselves jobs.* The curtain twitched before the door swung wide. Chris's face was a picture.

"Mr Finch," he said, clearly shocked.

Frankie pulled his best apologetic face, trying not to show his frustration at having waited around for two hours. But apologetic didn't come naturally to Frankie.

"Sorry to turn up unannounced. Wondered if you fancied a pint? There's something I need to run past you."

Chris's mouth stretched into a grimace. "I'm sorry, Mr Finch. I can't really leave mum. She's not well right now, and I've only just got in. Will a cup of tea do instead?"

Frankie shrugged, he wasn't used to people refusing him, but that would do. "That'd be great Chris, thanks."

As Chris put the kettle on, Frankie took in the small interior of the flat. It was clean and tidy but really run down. The lino in the kitchen was worn down to the concrete floor in places, and when Chris opened the fridge to grab some milk, it was almost empty. Frankie knew they weren't well off, but was surprised to see just how much they were struggling.

A breathless voice came from the next room. "Who is it, Christopher?"

"A friend from the gym, mum,"

"Well, don't be shy, bring him in so I can meet him."

Chris mouthed *Sorry* at Frankie, who chuckled and held both palms out in surrender.

Frankie followed him into the living room where his mum sat in an armchair with a blanket across her knees. Frankie had to hide his shock. Chris had said she wasn't well, but he'd neglected to mention just how ill she was. Her complexion was pale and sallow, and the skin sagged on her bones. She looked at death's door. But her personality hadn't dimmed any. She smiled up at Frankie with a glint in her eyes.

"My, you're a big lad aren't you? I bet you've been giving my Christopher a run for his money in the ring," she chuckled which gave way to a wheezing cough. She shooed Chris away with a shake of her hand. "Go on. That cup of tea won't make itself."

Chris looked exasperated and gave Frankie a helpless shrug, but he was smiling. He obviously loved his mum to bits. This must be tough on a young kid like him.

"How do you take your tea, Mr Finch?" He shouted back over the sound of the kettle boiling.

"Strong, three sugars," said Frankie, and heard Chris's mum tut with disapproval.

"Your teeth'll rot."

Frankie grinned, the woman had spirit. He liked that. She struggled forward in her chair and beckoned Frankie closer. She studied his face, eyes unwavering.

"I know who you are," she said. "And I need you to do something for me."

"Okay," said Frankie.

"It's Christopher. He's a good boy, and he's run ragged between working and looking after me." She paused as she took a few laboured breaths. Frankie started to rise to get Chris, but she waved him away impatiently. "Sit down; I haven't finished. I won't be here for much longer; I'm nearly done. And that boy's going to take it hard when I go. He hasn't got anyone else."

She put a hand over Frankie's, her skin papery. "I need you to promise me you'll look out for him. To have his back once I'm gone." She took a few more breaths. "I'm worried he'll go off the rails, do something stupid."

Frankie ignored the irony of her asking him to keep Chris on the straight and narrow. You took the words of a dying woman seriously. He nodded. "You have my word."

"Thank you." She slumped back in the armchair, her energy expended, and closed her eyes. Frankie's stomach lurched, *Oh shit, she hadn't just died, had she?* But then one eye flicked open, and she nodded her head almost imperceptibly towards the kitchen, "Go on, off you go."

Frankie smiled and gave her hand a gentle squeeze.

Chris was stirring sugar into the tea when Frankie walked back into the kitchen.

"Sorry about that," he said, his voice low. "She doesn't get to meet many new people."

"No problem, she's got some spirit has your mum."

"Oh no, was she giving you a hard time?"

Frankie chuckled. Then they both jumped as there was a loud thumping on the front door and shouts from outside. Nasty words, threats, insults, Frankie guessed from the stairwell kids. He was immediately in fighting mode. He glanced over at Chris, ready to go and teach them a lesson, but Chris was still leaning against the kitchen counter, a look of resignation on his face.

"You get that a lot?"

"All the time. It's just what it's like around here."

"Someone needs to take those kids in hand."

"It's not worth it. I used to think like that, but I can't be here all the time, and if I stand up to them, it just makes things worse for mum when she's here by herself."

Frankie took a sip of tea as he processed this. *Perfect. There was nothing like a decent cuppa.*

"So your mum's here by herself all day?"

"Yes, but it's OK. I get her breakfast and lunch sorted before I go to work. We manage," he said, and Frankie detected a note of defensiveness in his tone.

"I'm sure. There are no carers that come in?"

"No, mum won't have it. She says she's fine and doesn't want strangers fussing over her." Chris sighed. "But more and more lately I think she does need someone checking on her."

"Have you considered moving?"

Chris snorted. "We can barely afford this, Frankie. Besides we're OK, we manage."

Frankie took another sip of his tea.

"Why don't you come and work for me? I'd pay better than that warehouse job, and I could arrange for someone to look after your mum while you're at work. Or move you somewhere safer."

Chris hesitated. "I appreciate that Mr Finch but I couldn't do that. Besides, what would I be doing? I can't work nights or irregular hours. I know I'm not earning much at the moment, but it's a steady job and, no offence, but it's honest work."

Frankie nodded. The boy was proud and didn't want to accept help. He respected that. But all the same, he wanted to do something. Not just for Chris's sake, the mum obviously could do with some kind of care, but also because he wanted the kid on board. He'd be a useful asset.

"Well, think about it. The offer's there. And that's why I'm here actually. I wanted to ask your opinion about something."

19
HOLLYWOOD HUSTLE

Pandora was buzzing with excitement. The day of the engagement party had finally arrived. She'd been planning and looking forward to this for weeks.

Frankie had offered to throw the party at the club, which was ideal since the money from her movie role had long since dried up. Her overdraft was looming large on the horizon, especially without any other work on the cards. Clay was on a good salary, and they were mostly spending their time together in bed, which saved money, but after splurging on the engagement ring even he was pretty tapped out. In short, there was no way they could throw a lavish party without Frankie's help.

Once she discovered she wasn't footing the bill, Pandora had gone to town. She insisted on the party being themed. After lengthy discussions with Angie about how to maximise publicity, they decided on an Old Hollywood theme: the era of studio glamour, scandal and great gangster movies. They could have some fun with that, dress up and look fabulous and it would get the papers talking. The two of them had spent ages poring over old movies and photos of Hollywood legends to get costume and decoration ideas. It was going to be amazing.

Pandora started getting ready mid-afternoon. She needed to look her very best for this evening, so she shooed a bemused Clay out of the flat. *How would it take her so long to get ready?* His costume pretty much just involved him putting on a suit which would take less than five minutes. But Pandora was insistent.

She and Angie had run through the agency's contact list, and between them and Frankie, they'd put together an impressive guest list. Which was good since neither Pandora nor Clay had enough close friends to fill a large venue. Bea was really Pandora's only close friend, and most of Clay's mates already worked at the club. Clay's mum was the only other person coming, and Pandora wished she wasn't. She dreaded to think what the woman would be wearing. Glamorous she was not.

Angie had sweet-talked an upcoming fashion designer into making a dress, especially for Pandora. He was also loaning her a luxurious white faux fur jacket for the occasion. A hairdresser was booked for 5pm to set Pandora's platinum blonde hair in finger waves, so coupled with dark red Cupid's bow lips she'd look just like Jean Harlow.

Frankie had pulled out all the stops; he even laid on a limo for them. After all, it wasn't often that he got to fill the club with an A- the only flesh on show list crowd. At 7.45pm it pulled up outside Pandora's flat and Clay stepped out. She looked out through the window and smiled down at him. Looking every inch the gangster in his dark pinstripe suit, he really was spectacularly handsome. He ran up the stairs two at a time, and she was waiting at the open door to greet him. He stopped dead in his tracks when he saw her.

She gave an uncharacteristically shy smile. Would he like what she was wearing? With her old Hollywood makeover, she looked very different to normal. As a slow smile spread across his face relief washed over her. Phew, that was the effect she wanted to have. Tonight she needed to shine.

Her dress was a gold satin sheath with thin straps and a draped neckline which was cut to hug her every curve. It was simple, even demure compared to some of her other outfits - it wasn't low-cut, it didn't flash an enormous amount of leg, in fact, the only flesh on show was her arms, neck and ankles, but it was draped over her body like liquid gold, and she looked sensational. With every movement, you were aware of her body shifting beneath the dress. It was incredibly sexy. The rest of her outfit was simple, just a pair of gold heels and no jewellery except for that enormous rock of an engagement ring.

"Wow," breathed Clay sliding his hands around her waist. "I really am the luckiest man in the world."

Clay was wearing a Bogart-style suit with a fedora and looked like a gritty detective from a film noir. He had no idea who Humphrey Bogart was, but he'd let Pandora and Angie organise all that. As long as he didn't have to dress up in something stupid, he was happy. This was just another suit after all, and he kind of liked the hat. He wore it tilted forward at a rakish angle.

She grinned back at him and shivered as he dropped a kiss on her bare shoulder.

"Mmm, I love this dress, it feels amazing," he said, his hands sliding over the silk, feeling the warmth of her body beneath, his eyes sparkling with mischief.

She laughed and wriggled away. "I haven't spent all afternoon getting ready so you can muss me up before we even get there!"

Clay reluctantly shook his head. "OK, but we might have to leave early. I don't know how long I can keep my hands off you looking like that."

Over Pandora's shoulder, Clay spotted Bea perched

nervously on the sofa.

"Bea, you look lovely," he said. She knew Clay was just being polite, but she liked him for it. He was kind. She knew that next to Pandora she looked ordinary, but she was used to that. Still, she was excited about this evening. She'd bought a new dress and was looking forward to seeing Stanley. Not that she'd get to see him very much. With it being Clay's party Stanley had been bumped up the chain of command and was in charge tonight, something he was taking very seriously. She hoped it went well for him. The downside, of course, was that Bea would have to make her own way to the party. That was fine, she was a big girl, but she was out of her comfort zone and would have loved him by her side.

She watched Pandora fussing around looking for her handbag, and shook her head. She would never have had the nerve to wear a dress like that, and besides she didn't have Pandora's spectacular figure. But she'd splashed out and dipped into her savings to buy a new dress for this evening. It was wine red with lace sleeves and a sweetheart neckline. It fell to just above the knee and showed off her slim legs. Bea was also wearing contacts instead of glasses for the first time in public. She'd been practising with them for the past week, trying to get used to them, but they still felt a little scratchy. She just hoped she'd be able to last the evening in them. Her glasses were in her handbag just in case.

Since Stanley couldn't take her, Bea was going in the limo with Clay, Pandora and Angie. At least there was a group of them, so she wasn't too much of a spare wheel. For all Pandora's assurances, Bea knew as soon as Pandora saw flashbulbs she'd be totally forgotten, but that was fair enough, it was her party after all, and Pandora wasn't there to babysit her.

Angie joined them dressed in a men's suit, with a pencilled-in moustache and slicked-back hair. The look suited her.

"Shall we?" she said, offering Bea her arm, and Bea giggled. This was going to be fun.

20
RULES OF ENGAGEMENT

Since the club was closed to the public, there wasn't the usual queue outside. In fact, the only sign of life was Big Arf standing out front. As soon as they stepped out of the limo, he swung the door open, giving Bea a small bow as she passed. She giggled, it felt like she was in on some wonderful secret.

The stairs were edged with scattered red rose petals leading up, like a red carpet but with a path in the middle, so you didn't get petals stuck to the soles of your shoes. And to her delight on every landing, there was an actor dressed as a character from a movie. She gazed wide-eyed as Indiana Jones offered her his arm for the walk up. "I hope we don't come across any large boulders rolling towards us" she whispered, blushing furiously. Her guide smiled at her but was silent; she suspected he looked the part but couldn't do an American accent. He escorted her to the top floor, where he kissed her hand and then headed back down to re-take his original position.

As Pandora and Clay entered the club, a huge cheer went up. They had timed their arrival to make an entrance, so the room was already full. Cameras flashed and the happy couple posed for photos, clutching one another and looking every bit in love.

Bea and Angie sneaked past, and Bea stopped short when she saw the club. It looked incredible. *Stanley had done a great job,* she thought proudly. The club always looked glamorous, but tonight it had been transformed from a tropical oasis into somewhere befitting an Oscars after-party. The tables had elaborate ostrich-feather centrepieces, and there were bits of borrowed film sets and props around the edges of the room, zoning the club into different styles. One area was Egyptian themed with a pyramid backdrop and golden statues of Egyptian gods; another was set in Ancient Rome with pillars looking like the inside of Caesar's palace. Then there was what looked like a rainforest complete with King Kong, which stood right next to a Broadway street scene. *Wow.*

A girl in a vintage-style cigarette girl uniform asked Bea if she could take her jacket, and Bea shyly shrugged off her ever-practical woollen coat, the only one she owned. The girl flashed her a kind smile and handed her a ticket.

As Bea looked around, she saw all the female staff were dressed as cigarette girls, their hair set in waves and wearing red lipstick. They must have had a hairdresser here getting them ready all afternoon. Bea suddenly felt conscious that she'd done nothing more than brush her hair and add the pretty diamanté clip Stanley had given her.

Some of the girls had cigarette trays around their necks which were filled with delicious looking canapés, and there were pyramids of champagne glasses sparkling and glinting on the bar. *What a cool party,* thought Bea. Never in her wildest dreams did she think she'd get to go to something like this.

She felt a hand on her arm and realised she'd been standing gaping.

"Come on, let's get some drinks, I'm gasping!" said

Angie with a wink. "No point just standing there. Dive in, have some fun!"

Bea glanced over to Pandora, who was air-kissing and saying her hellos to everyone. She was in her element.

"What can I get you, ladies?" smiled the girl behind the bar. Her hair was white blonde and styled perfectly to match her outfit, but the colour seemed too harsh for her, the gash of red lipstick only emphasising her pallor. The girl smiled politely, but Bea saw a sadness behind her eyes and felt a pang of pity. *It was such a lovely evening. Why did she look so miserable?*

Angie, of course, noticed no such thing, she ordered drinks and returned to scan the room. *Like a panther on the prowl,* thought Bea.

She spotted Stanley across the room, and he waved at her, his face splitting into a grin. She waved back, and he came over. *He always looked so smart at work,* she thought proudly. Kissing her on the cheek, he told Bea she looked beautiful.

He was sweet. She knew she couldn't compete with the other women in the room, she was like a sparrow surrounded by birds of paradise, but it was sweet of him to say so. They chatted for a few moments, but she could see he was watching the room the whole time to make sure everything was okay. There would be no calamities on his watch.

She knew the party was a big deal for him. Being second in command he rarely got any credit for his hard work, but since Clay was the guest of honour today he had been in charge of the whole evening, and she knew it was important that it went well. Plus Frankie was here, so the pressure was on.

She squeezed his hand. "Go on, you go and get on; I know how busy you are."

"I'll come and find you later, OK? Save me a dance?"

She nodded, and he walked briskly off.

Bea and Angie went over to their table. They had seats

at the central table along with the happy couple and Frankie and Linda Finch who were already seated.

Frankie wasn't one for dressing up. In fact, he looked exactly the same as usual, but with the addition of a red a carnation in his buttonhole to make him the Godfather. Linda, on the other hand, had gone the full Marilyn Monroe. A petite woman with long dark hair, her transformation was startling, but she carried it off surprisingly well. Her dark hair was hidden underneath a platinum blonde wig, and she was wearing that famous white halterneck dress. She rose and gave Bea a hug.

"Wow, you look gorgeous", Linda said, then in an undertone, "Stanley is one lucky guy."

Bea smiled shyly, her eyes round. She was surprised Stanley had mentioned they were going out.

"Thanks, you're very kind. You look amazing, Mrs Finch,"

"Oh, call me Linda! Mrs Finch sounds like my mother-in-law," she said with an exaggerated groan. "Besides," she patted her hair and squeezed her red lips into a play pout, "tonight I'm Marilyn. You like?"

Bea laughed. "Perfect!" she said.

Pandora was in seventh heaven. The first hour of the party was a whirlwind of hellos and hugs, with anyone and everyone wanting to congratulate them. Even Pandora was slightly star-struck by some of the people Angie had managed to get to the party. But there was still work to be done before they could relax.

Angie tapped Pandora on the shoulder and whispered that it was time for their interview. She'd arranged for a celebrity magazine to cover the party, and the reporter was waiting for them on the private balcony. Clay scowled, wanting to relax and enjoy the party. He hadn't even had a bloody drink yet.

The reporter was a tight-faced middle-aged woman wearing a tweed suit and frilly blouse. She looked rather stuffy compared to the peacocks around her, more suited to a shooting party with the country set than a showbiz bash. But then Edie Easterbrook was working; she wasn't here to play. And it would do Pandora well to remember that. The woman was a formidable reporter with a nose for scandal, infamous for sniffing out any dirty little secrets, which she would then hold on file, giving her the power to release a damning exposé if she ever took a dislike to you. She was both the most revered and hated woman in the British celebrity press.

As the makeup girl touched up Pandora's face, Edie had an informal chat with Clay, who had little experience of talking to journalists. However, he knew this was important to Pandora, and he was in full-on charm mode, despite still being desperate for a drink.

Pandora strained to hear what they were saying. Edie opened with a couple of innocuous questions about how the pair met and their plans for the wedding. Clay was saying all the right things, and Pandora began to relax. Until she heard questioning take on a more probing tone.

"So, how did you get your scar, Mr Caulder? My readers will be dying to know?"

Clay chuckled indulgently. He wasn't surprised she was intrigued, most people were, and he had little idea how savage the press could be. "Ah well, let's just say it was a disagreement."

"So it was a fight?"

"I don't want to go into detail, but let's just say the other guy didn't get off so lightly."

But Edie had scented a story and wasn't prepared to let the matter drop. She changed tack. "How old were you at the time?"

"I said I don't want to talk about it."

"But Mr Caulder, you simply can't hold out on me," she said, putting her hand on his knee and simpering, "my readers will be desperate to know. A scar on a handsome man is always so intriguing."

Clay looked at her levelly, all trace of banter gone. "I was fourteen."

Edie tried to hide her shock. She hadn't expected that.

Clay raised his eyebrows, daring her to ask more. But Edie was made of tougher stuff and barely missed a beat.

"So, what did you do to the other guy?"

Pandora, who could hear the conversation, gestured frantically to Angie to intervene but Angie just shrugged. *After all, any publicity was good publicity.*

Pandora felt her frustration rising; she was pinned by the makeup artist who was busy fussing about with her eye shadow and kept telling her not to move. "Hurry up," she hissed.

"Perfection," the girl replied, tongue sticking between her teeth in concentration, "takes patience. Or do you want to be photographed half-done?" She was under strict instructions to keep Pandora busy while the reporter talked to Clay.

Meanwhile, Clay, who had realised Edie was just after a scandal, slid his usual mask back into place and ramped up the charm. He gave her a warm smile. "Let's just say that's ancient history. Now, aren't we supposed to be talking about this upcoming wedding?"

The reporter tinkled a laugh but made a mental note to go searching through police and court reports. It sounded like there was a story to be had. And one with juicy details. It could add a real edge of steel to what would otherwise be just another fluffy celebrity engagement piece. Especially if Clay had killed or maimed someone. They might even be able to get a quote from the victim or the victim's family. And even if she didn't use it now, it would definitely come in handy in the future.

Finally, Pandora was released from the makeup chair, and she sashayed over to perch on Clay's lap, flashing the reporter a huge smile and instantly taking control. She needed to get this interview back on track and all about her and her career.

Ivy stood behind the bar watching the photoshoot through narrowed eyes.

I bet Clay loves all this, she thought sourly. *He'd always been vain and full of himself; he must love being a minor celebrity. Although I bet he doesn't like playing second fiddle to his fiancée.*

She shook herself in irritation. Why was she being so down on him? Clay looked happy, and he was her friend. She should try to be happy for him. She just wished he were happy with someone who wasn't such a bitch.

I wonder how Frankie feels about all this attention, she mused. Although glancing over in Frankie's direction, she had to admit he looked pretty chuffed. He loved the increased publicity the couple were bringing to the club, so everyone was happy. Everyone, that was, except her. That was, so long as increased publicity didn't bring with it increased scrutiny. The club itself was a reputable business; it was the more shadowy side of his operations that Frankie wouldn't want the press looking into.

Her heart lurched, and she looked away as Clay and Pandora kissed on the balcony for the camera. *They're perfect for one another,* she thought despairingly. *I was kidding myself that he could ever be happy with me.*

Frankie, who had been standing across the bar for the last minute or so cleared his throat. She jumped to attention. "Am I interrupting something, Ivy?"

"Sorry Mr Finch," she said, her cheeks flaming. "What can I get you?"

"Could you bring over a tray of cocktails, please? A general selection. Linda's convinced everyone to try something a bit different."

Ivy nodded and got to work, making the drinks. She wanted to get them delivered to the table before Clay and Pandora got back.

Sadly though, making a tray of cocktails takes time, especially when each one is a miniature masterpiece, and by the time she had finished, the happy couple had returned to the table.

Ivy loaded up the tray. She felt ridiculous in this costume. The skirt stuck out with lots of net and was way too short. Plus she'd been given seamed tights to wear underneath. Instead of feeling sexy, she just felt a bit slutty. She snorted, *at least Clay should like it then.* Not that he noticed anything about her any more. She was the invisible woman. The outfit was something she'd never dream of wearing, but what choice did she have? All the staff were having to wear them tonight, the female staff anyway. Despite her mood, a smile briefly tugged her lips at the thought of the men being forced to wear them as well. A mental picture of Big Arf wearing the outfit popped into her head, and she stifled a giggle. That was a picture that would stay with her for a while.

She slapped a weary smile on her face and went over. As she leant forward to put the tray of drinks on the table, she felt a hand snake up the back of her thigh. She shrieked in surprise, and the tray toppled. She turned furiously to see who it was, and was about to shout at the man when she was distracted by a loud shriek. Ivy turned, and her face fell as she realised what she had done. Most of the drinks had landed in Pandora's lap.

Pandora was furious, and everyone at the table had jumped up and was trying to help. Her clingy satin dress was now slicked wet against her skin, the cocktails leaving a huge wet stain on the gold satin. She looked like she wanted to go berserk, but aware of the magazine photographer snapping away she didn't want to give them any ammunition, so she silently allowed Clay to lead her off to the office.

"Clean this bloody mess up," he barked furiously over his shoulder at Ivy.

As she bent down to start picking up pieces of glass, tears brimming in her eyes, Ivy noticed that Linda had a big splodge of red on her Marilyn dress.

"Oh, I'm so sorry, Mrs Finch," she said mortified.

"Don't you worry Ivy," smiled Linda. "I saw exactly what happened." She leaned over to the guy who was smirking as he watched Ivy clean up.

"You can piss off you little creep. I saw what you did, and if I see you lay another hand on her I'll break your fingers, understand?"

The smirk vanished, and he looked shocked, unsure how to react. Linda gave him a shooing gesture. "Go on, piss off," she said, eyebrow raised.

Ivy smiled gratefully and mouthed "thanks."

Just then everybody's attention was diverted as the floor show started with a spectacular fire act, which was a mixture of daring and spectacle. The guests were swiftly distracted from looking over at the aftermath of the cocktail disaster, allowing Ivy to finish clearing up and then head to the bathroom to try and sponge the spill off her own outfit.

"That silly little bitch has always had it in for me," stormed Pandora, rage pouring out now she was out of public view.

"I don't think so, baby," soothed Clay.

Pandora looked hurt. "You wouldn't know. You've always had a blind spot when it comes to bloody Ivy. I haven't said anything to you before now; I didn't want to cause trouble. But she's been constantly making nasty comments to me whenever you're not around. I bet she did this on purpose to ruin our special night."

"Really?" said Clay. *That didn't sound like Ivy at all.* Perhaps Pandora had got the wrong end of the stick. Besides, maybe this wasn't so bad. He'd wanted to get her alone all evening. "Now what are we going to do about this dress?" He ran a hand up her side. "I really think we need to get you out of it," he said with a glint in his eye, his hand wandering up to cup her breast.

Pandora slapped his hand away.

"Seriously Clay, I'm not in the fucking mood. I want

that girl fired. I've had enough of her trying to sabotage everything we do."

Clay's eyes narrowed. *That was a bit extreme.* "I'll talk to her tomorrow."

"No," said Pandora, "you get rid of her now. Or don't you want to because of the history you two have? Do you still like her? She's got you wound around her little finger, and you don't even realise it." A tear rolled down Pandora's cheek, and she pouted. Clay was horrified. *Perhaps Pandora was right; perhaps Ivy did have it in for her. She had been acting weird recently. Was it out of jealousy?*

"I want her gone by the time I get back out of here. I'm not giving her the satisfaction of being able to laugh at the trouble she's caused me. Give me your jacket so I can get out of this dress. I'm bloody freezing. And get my coat for me. I'll just have to wear that instead."

Clay handed his jacket over and strode back out into the club, anger boiling in his veins. How dare Ivy be nasty to Pandora? Nobody was horrible to his fiancée and got away with it.

It was ten minutes later when Clay walked back into the office to find Pandora leaning against the desk wearing his suit jacket, arms folded across her chest.

"So?" she demanded.

"Done," he said. "She's gone."

Pandora's face relaxed into a smile. That was an added bonus; she was sick of Ivy always mooning around after Clay. *Good riddance to bad rubbish.*

She unfolded her arms, and the jacket fell open, revealing she was naked underneath.

Clay's eyes took in the view, and he dropped her coat onto a chair, sliding his arms inside the jacket and sighing as he felt her warm skin beneath his hands. He'd wanted to do this ever since he saw her in that dress. The spill might have been a disaster, but perhaps it wasn't all bad.

He moved to kiss her, but she ducked her face away,

giving him her neck instead. "Not the face baby, I don't want to smudge my make up."

Clay smiled and shook his head. *Women were strange creatures.* Still, he could work with that, as long as nowhere else was out of bounds. He slid the jacket off her shoulders, trailing kisses slowly downwards until he reached her parted legs. He looked up at her as her head rocked back and smiled to himself. This magnificent woman was all his. He truly was the luckiest man alive.

Frankie raised his eyebrows in amazement. Pandora could turn even a disaster into a masterclass in self-promotion. He grinned as she walked out onto the floor wearing a white fur coat, heels and probably nothing else, he couldn't help it. That girl was as bold as brass. A natural-born publicity magnet.

He looked at Linda, who rolled her eyes. She obviously wasn't keen, but then she was probably thinking personally rather than in terms of getting press coverage.

Once again, Pandora had managed to steal everyone's attention. She was surrounded by a small crowd and was giving the photographer yet more ammunition. *Atta girl,* thought Frankie.

His phone rang, and he glanced at the screen.

"Yes?" he barked, irritated at being interrupted on a night out.

He frowned. "Hold on there, slow down," he said, getting up and striding over to the balcony to get some quiet.

"Say again, Chris? I couldn't hear you."

Frankie listened intently his jaw clenched. "Stay where you are. I'll be right there."

He marched back into the room, whispered something into Linda's ear and within a minute, he was gone.

21
DEATH IN THE FAMILY

When Frankie arrived at Chris's place, it took every ounce of willpower not to turn and walk away. Police cars were everywhere; blue lights illuminating the darkness. Not a scene he would usually willingly walk into. But this wasn't a usual night. Frankie saw a man in a white forensics suit walking towards the flat, and his lips pressed together.

He scanned the crowd and spotted a familiar figure leaning against a police car, staring blankly into space.

Frankie put his hand on the boy's shoulder. Chris turned to him, his face distraught.

"Sorry, Mr Finch, I shouldn't have called you away from your party. I didn't know who else to call. I'm going to have to go down the station in a minute anyway."

"What? They can't seriously think you did this," Frankie gestured to the bustling crime scene.

Chris shrugged. "Dunno. They need to ask questions, I guess. It's not like I can refuse to go."

"Have you got a lawyer?"

"What do you think?" Chris snorted, then shook his head and let out a sigh. "Sorry, Mr Finch, I didn't mean to be rude. Besides, I don't need a lawyer. Once they check with work, they'll know it wasn't me. I just walked in and found her. But I've still got to go through everything with them."

Frankie nodded, then lowered his voice. "Have you got any idea who did this?"

"It'll be those same fucking kids. She called the police on them yesterday cos they were causing trouble, and they said they were going to get her." His voice broke as emotion overcame him. "I didn't think for a moment she was really in danger."

His voice trailed off, and he watched in silent horror as a body bag was wheeled out on a gurney. He let out a strangled howl. Frankie's face hardened. He couldn't believe the little shits had done this.

A young police officer approached. "Come with us please Mr Slaughter. We need you to come down the station. Step into the back of the car, please."

Frankie blocked his path.

"He knows who did this, did he tell you? Have you arrested them yet?"

The policeman raised an eyebrow as he recognised Frankie. "We're making enquiries Mr Finch, but first we need to take Mr Slaughter's statement."

"Come on, lad. You know how this works. They'll be getting rid of evidence, skipping town. You need to get after them. Chris knows where they live, right?"

Chris nodded.

The policeman said, a little patronisingly, "I'm sure you know how this works too Mr Finch. You don't need to worry about that. We're investigating. Let us take it from here."

Chris turned to Frankie with a resigned look on his face as he got into the back of the police car.

"Thanks for coming Mr Finch, I appreciate it."

"Which police station are you taking him to?"

"Bethnal Green, sir."

He leant down to speak to Chris, "I'll be there when they release you." But before Chris could respond, the car door was shut, and the police car pulled away.

Frankie wanted nothing more right now than to find the little fuckers who had done this, but he couldn't do a thing while the place was crawling with police, so he needed to focus on Chris. He took one last look at the crazy circus and clenched his fists. They wouldn't get away with this.

Dawn light was struggling through the thick London cloud by the time Chris was released. He looked shocked and exhausted.

He'd had to go over and over the events of that evening like some awful recurring nightmare. But there wasn't much he could tell them. He'd gone to work, had come straight home on the bus, and he'd arrived home to find the front door kicked in and his mum in a pool of congealed blood in her armchair. By then, she was cold and had clearly been dead for some time. The carpet around her feet was saturated, and she sat with her hair tilted back, mouth gaping, eyes staring unseeing at the ceiling. An image that would live with Chris forever.

He was surprised to find Frankie sitting in reception when he emerged, but he felt so numb and tired that he was just grateful to climb into the car and get out of there. He couldn't think straight. It was like his brain had shut down with shock. Frankie took him to the Brew n Chew and with one nod to the exit, the place emptied. The last man out turned the sign on the door to closed.

"Right, tell me what happened."

Chris shrugged. "They just kept going over it again and again," he said bleakly. "But what could I tell them? I was at work; I went home, I found her. I told them who must have done it, but they seemed more interested in what I'd been doing."

"Well, they released you, so you can't be a suspect."

Frankie leaned back as the waitress brought them two mugs of strong tea. "Get a tot of brandy to go in that too love."

Frankie stirred sugar into the teas and added a generous splash of alcohol to Chris's. The boy was in shock. He pushed a mug over to Chris, who wrapped his hands around it and stared blankly down.

"Come on, lad, get that inside you. It'll do you good."

Frankie took a sip and sighed. It had been a long night, and police station tea was always terrible. A decent cuppa never failed to raise his mood. He watched Chris, who was staring into his mug, unmoving.

"I know you don't feel like drinking it, but it'll help. Trust me."

Chris stood suddenly, his chair scraping harshly against the floor, tea slopping onto the table.

His eyes wild Chris said, "Thanks for everything you've done Mr Finch, but I need to get back there. I can't just sit here; I need to find the bastards who did this."

Frankie put a restraining arm on Chris's shoulder and wondered briefly whether he would have a fight on his hands. But after a moment of resistance, Chris seemed to crumple, and Frankie eased him back into his seat.

"Believe me, that's the last thing you need to do right now. The place is crawling with police, and going after some kids right now will just get you banged up."

"I don't care," he said, a desperate defiance in his voice.

"I know you don't right now, Chris. And I totally get that, but you need to hold back. Trust me when I say we'll sort this. You have my word. But now isn't the time to be taking matters into your own hands."

Chris nodded, the fight draining from him, and slowly took a sip of tea.

The waitress arrived and slid two steaming plates of breakfast in front of them. Chris blanched at the sight of food and pushed his plate away, but Frankie dived in. There was nothing like a good fry-up after a night in a police station. He was starving.

"Now, have you got somewhere to stay?"

Chris frowned and then grief flooded him again as he realised he wouldn't be allowed back to the flat. Not while it was a crime scene. He shook his head, blinking away tears.

"Right, you're coming home with me then."

"I couldn't."

"Course you could. Besides where else are you going to go?"

Chris shrugged. There was nowhere else. Frankie was right. "OK, thanks," he mumbled.

Frankie felt terrible for the kid. This was a shitty thing to happen, and it was going to be difficult stopping him from taking matters into his own hands. Taking him home was the only way Frankie could think of preventing that.

Frankie never slept in. His body clock woke him around 6am regardless of the time he went to bed, but the following morning he didn't open his eyes till nearly 10. Still groggy, he stumbled towards the guest room to see if Chris was up yet.

He frowned. The bed was made, and the room was immaculate. Almost like it hadn't been slept in at all, but that couldn't be right. Chris must have crashed out at least for a bit.

He padded downstairs, dreading the reception he'd get. He hadn't told Linda they had a house guest, so fully expected an earful. She must have had the fright of her life when Chris walked in.

He found Linda sitting at the kitchen table squinting at her laptop. She glanced up at him.

"Hello babe, you had a late one last night."

He gave her a sleepy kiss on the head and went to pour himself a coffee.

"Yeah, a really late one. Where's Chris?"

"Who?"

That woke Frankie up. "What, you mean he isn't here?"

"Who isn't here?"

He dashed around the house, sticking his head into every room, but they were all empty. Then he spotted a note on the hall table.

He opened it, swore quietly and bolted upstairs to get dressed. This was the last thing he fucking needed.

In record time he was out the door and reversing the car out of the driveway.

Linda, who had long since got used to Frankie's strange hours and random behaviour, shook her head and went back to the screen. It was best not to ask questions. She only got given vague excuses anyway. Besides, Frankie knew what he was doing, and they were both happier when she just left him to it.

Frankie dialled Chris as he drove, but the call went to voicemail. He pressed the accelerator harder. He knew where Chris would be.

He dived down side streets, honking his horn at unsuspecting pedestrians, avoiding the traffic as well as any London cabbie, and soon he reached the estate. Abandoning the car he jogged in, looking around. There was no sign of Chris. An old biddy was wheeling a shopping trolley across the courtyard, and some kids were playing football, but other than that everything was quiet. Frankie ran upstairs towards the third floor flat. There was a lone policeman outside, and the crime scene tape was still in place. *OK, so Chris wasn't there. Where the hell was he?* Frankie leaned over the balcony, frustrated and tried Chris's phone again.

It went straight to voicemail. *Was his battery flat? Or was he avoiding Frankie's call?*

The corner of his eye caught a figure skirting the edge of the courtyard which disappeared around the corner. Frankie broke into a run, dashing down the piss-smelling stairwell until he reached the ground floor. He heard shouting and headed towards it. Rounding the corner, he found Chris looming over a figure on the floor.

"Where is he?" Chris snarled, his fist balled in a teenage boy's t-shirt holding his shoulders an inch off the ground.

"Chris!"

He glanced up, and Frankie shook his head in warning. With a shove, he released the kid who scrambled to his feet and pulled a knife.

"Oh, for fuck's sake, put that away and go home," said Frankie.

"You don't get to tell me what to do."

Frankie's eyes narrowed. "Don't push me today you mouthy little shit."

The kid didn't like this and lunged towards Frankie, his knife flashing. Frankie, who'd guessed this was coming and who had the benefit of greater experience and a longer reach, knocked the knife out of the kid's hand. With a sharp jab under the chin and a knee to the balls, he left the kid lying dazed and groaning on the floor.

Frankie bent down and pocketed the knife, then gave the kid a shove with his foot.

"Get the fuck out of here."

The kid scrabbled to his knees and limped off muttering curses under his breath.

When he reached a safe distance, he shouted, "You're dead grandad, fucking dead. I'm in with much more important people than you. You think you're so fucking big, but you're not running things around here any more."

"Oh yeah, who is then?"

"If you don't know already, you'll know soon enough. They're coming for you old man."

Frankie rolled his eyes.

"Is that the kid who did it?"

"One of that same gang, but I don't think it was actually him. He was mouthing off, saying his mate did it. Said she deserved it. I could so easily have killed him, Frankie, why did you stop me?"

Frankie slung his arm around Chris's shoulders.

"I know how angry you are, how much you want to kick the shit out of someone. I know how that feels. But going after the kids who did this in broad daylight when the place is crawling with police, isn't the way to do it."

He put his hands on either side of Chris's face to make sure he was listening. "I made a promise to your mum that I'd keep you out of trouble. And I intend to keep that promise. Which includes making sure you don't get banged up for going after those little shits. Understand?" Chris nodded. "I'll sort this. But you need to trust me. Those little fuckers will pay. But you're not going down for it, understand?

"Let's get out of here and go down the gym. You need to get some of that anger out of your system. And once you've knackered yourself out, have a big breakfast, half a bottle of whiskey and go to bed. It's a much better option than getting yourself banged up. Do you trust me to sort this for you?"

Chris nodded. If he trusted anyone right now, it was Frankie.

"Right let's go hit something."

22
A DELICATE STANDOFF

Frankie spent the next week making sure Chris didn't bolt or go off the rails, which he achieved in no small part thanks to Linda. Once he explained the circumstances she'd immediately taken charge, her mothering instinct going into full swing. Linda was totally bossing him around, and luckily Chris was smart enough to know when he'd met his match. She made sure he was eating properly and kept him busy doing long-neglected jobs around the house and helping out with the kids.

Linda decided that if Chris was staying with them for more than a couple of days, he could do with his own space. Their spare room was great when her mum came to stay, but it was a bit too pink and floral for a grown lad. Frankie had agreed, but even that slight degree of separation made him nervous that Chris might do a runner. So they had spent the last couple of days clearing out the junk room over the garage, decorating it and turning it into a bedroom.

In the meantime, Frankie was true to his word. Chris had packed in his warehouse job and was now officially on his payroll, although any actual work was on hold until after the funeral. That was good since Frankie had no idea what Chris would be doing. He valued the lad's take on things and was glad to have him on board, but with the promise he'd made Chris's mum echoing in his ears, he couldn't involve him in anything high-risk. He needed to keep the boy out of trouble, which, with his current trigger-fuse, would be tough enough without getting him doing something illegal.

Eventually, he came up with a plan that satisfied two needs: Chris's need for a job, and his increasing road rage when dealing with the heavy London traffic. He'd always fancied the idea of having a driver.

There was only one problem. Chris couldn't drive. He'd never passed his test. He'd never even had lessons. You didn't need to in London; everyone used the tube or the bus. Everyone, that was, except Frankie, who fucking hated public transport.

So he booked Chris on an intensive driving course, and when he passed his test, Frankie booked him onto an advanced course, getting him used to driving fast and in larger, more powerful cars. Besides, Frankie had to admit to being a touch nervous about being in the car with an inexperienced driver. He was too used to being in control.

Frankie's Jag was exclusively for his use, so Chris would be driving their black suped-up Range Rover. It was as tough as a tank and fast enough to get them out of any kind of trouble. So Chris, courses passed, got used to driving that, going out for a few hours of driving each day with a local cabbie, familiarising himself with all the local roads and routes he'd be using. The rest of the time, Linda was keeping him so busy he barely had time to think. Which was, of course, Linda's intention.

She knew how easy it was for boys to get themselves into trouble if they had time on their hands, especially when they were angry with the world. After all, she'd known Frankie at that age.

Meanwhile, Frankie had thoroughly quizzed him about the kid who'd killed his mum, wanting to know the whole history in minute detail: where he lived, where he hung out, rumours, previous incidents, and more about who he worked for. Which led back to the Albanians again.

But he couldn't let that stop him. Frankie had promised to sort this out, and he wouldn't let the small matter of starting a gang war stop him from getting retribution. He owed the kid that.

23
INTRODUCTIONS & INSECURITIES

Chris had been behind the wheel just shy of a month when Frankie finally got in the car with him. He needed to go out anyway, and it was about time they got used to this new arrangement. After all, there was no point him having Chris on the payroll if he wasn't going to use him for anything.

Frankie was pleasantly surprised by the uneventful ten-minute drive to the Club, during which his brake-foot only surged forward a couple of times. He would never have admitted that he was nervous about Chris's driving, but he clearly was.

Chris pulled up outside and glanced up, catching Frankie wince at the prospect of having his alloys curbed. But Chris parked beautifully, smiling to himself. He was all too aware of his boss's anxiety. He switched the engine off and looked up at the flashy sign for The Flamingo Club.

"I've heard about this place."

"You ever been in?"

Chris shook his head. "You're joking, aren't you, Mr Finch? When would I get the chance to hang out in a place like this?"

Frankie grinned. "Well, a driver would usually stay in the car, but since it's your first day come on in. I'll show you around."

They jogged up the stairs. Frankie refused on principle to take a lift. For one, the stairs kept you fit, but also he felt claustrophobic in a small metal box, cornered, with only one exit. Not a sensible position to get yourself in, even if you do own the building.

When they reached the top floor, they walked out onto the spacious roof terrace, and Chris's face lit up like a kid at Christmas. "Wow," he breathed, making Frankie chuckle. Chris might look big and tough, but he was still young underneath it all. And he was guessing there had been precious little wonder in his life. Plus, it was nice to know that palm trees, fountains and flamingos were still enough to impress the younger generation. Perhaps the place wasn't losing its appeal after all.

"Frankie!" Clay strode over and shook his hand.

"Clay, this is Chris." The two men shook hands, nodding respectfully at one another, Clay with the ghost of a frown on his face. *Frankie didn't usually bring people around, and this kid was new. Who the hell was he?*

It was mid-afternoon, and the club was getting ready for opening. Chairs stacked upside down on the tabletops were busy being righted, and candles in little glass jars were being put in the centre of each table. Frankie scanned the room. Everything looked in order. He nodded and raised his hand in recognition to a few people, stopping short when he looked over at the bar.

"How come Clementine's working the bar? Is Ivy not in tonight?"

Clay shrugged. "Ivy left."

"Really?" Frankie frowned. He didn't like it when staff left. Disgruntled employees caused problems. He liked stability and to know the people who were working for him were loyal. If people were leaving, that indicated a problem. And he didn't need any more problems right now.

"Why?"

'Honestly, Frankie? I told the clumsy cow to go. She's been causing too many issues recently. Plus she's got it in for Pandora. She spilt those drinks over her on purpose."

"Are you sure about that? Linda told me she got goosed.'

Clay rolled his eyes, "Yeah well, Ivy would say that, wouldn't she? She just can't stand to see how much everyone loves Pandora."

Frankie wasn't convinced. He suspected the decision had been made more by Pandora than Clay. He and Ivy had always got on well in the past; in fact, he'd always thought the two of them might end up together. She would have been a steadying influence on Clay. And if Pandora had spotted that she might well have caused trouble for Ivy.

He made a mental note to go and check on Ivy and hear her side of things. She didn't strike him as being unreliable, or one to walk out on a job. And it didn't ring true that she would have been fired for being a liability, she'd always been a conscientious girl. He suspected there was something Clay wasn't telling him, and Frankie wasn't a man who liked taking chances.

Clay meanwhile quickly turned the conversation round to the upcoming Christmas wedding. Frankie was letting them have the reception at the club, partly since it was good for business, but also because he suspected they couldn't afford to pay for it for themselves and he liked the idea of playing the benefactor. He paid Clay a good wage to run the club, not to mention a few extras for other little jobs, but he suspected it was all going on keeping Pandora happy. That woman was high maintenance. Besides, Frankie didn't mind. The publicity from the engagement party had been gold, and a celebrity wedding would be even better.

Having said that, he had zero interest in the details, and part of him wanted the wedding done and dusted so Clay could knuckle back down to his day job again.

He was starting to get increasingly irritated by Clay's constant distraction. It was understandable with this whirlwind romance going on, but he wasn't prepared to tolerate Clay's slack behaviour for much longer.

Despite the recent surge in interest the club had enjoyed, Frankie was all too aware of the work needed to maintain that. It was about attracting the right quality of customer. The club was full every night either way, but if you filled it with high-rolling rich people and celebs, you took double the money than if you filled it with regular punters. And achieving that was done by making those high-paying customers feel special. That was what Clay should be doing. Not getting fitted for a bloody suit and tasting wedding cakes.

Had he been the same when he and Linda got married? *Don't be fucking ridiculous,* he told himself. While it had been his idea to get married, their wedding had been completely organised by Linda and her mother. His job had just been to turn up on the day and put the ring on Linda's finger. And to pay for it all.

He thought fondly back to that day. They got hitched at the Town Hall and had a knees-up at the local pub afterwards, and it had been perfect. But trust Clay to want to go all-out for maximum effect. Although Frankie had to admit it would get in all the papers.

"Clay," he interrupted, bored of hearing about fucking wedding favours, "get Stanley for me, will you? I want to have a word."

"Sure boss," said Clay, happy to escape. He hadn't been expecting a drop-in from Frankie, and he'd promised Pandora he'd look over the seating plan for the reception before tonight.

He found Stanley wheeling crates of wine up from the

cellar.

"You're in trouble," he said with a smirk. "Boss wants to see you up top."

Stanley gulped, his eyes wide. "Why, what's he said?"

"Don't ask me. Take those upstairs; then, he wants to see you. I'd hurry though; I wouldn't keep Frankie waiting if I was you, not in the mood he's in."

Clay chuckled to himself as Stanley hurried anxiously away. *He was so easy to wind up.* Stanley was one of life's worriers and the absolute opposite to Clay, which made teasing him so easy, and so enjoyable, not least because he always fell for it. He needed to take a leaf out of Clay's book and loosen up a bit.

Stanley arrived at Frankie's table flushed and out of breath. Frankie looked up, surprised.

"You OK, Stan? You look a bit hot and bothered?"

"Yes, Mr Finch," he gasped, trying to regain his composure. "I was down in the basement, bringing some crates up, I came as quick as I could."

The corner of Frankie's mouth twitched. He liked that. Stanley might be as timid as a mouse, but he jumped when you called, and he could be relied on to do a proper job. Clay was a great front-man, but Stanley was the one who made sure the club ran smoothly.

"Sit down Stan."

Stanley pulled up a chair and perched on the edge of it, sweating slightly.

"What's up, Mr Finch?"

"I wanted to have a word. I've got something I want you to do for me." *Bless him; the kid looked nervous.* He's worried I want him to take someone out or something.

Frankie smiled reassuringly but only succeeded in looking more sharklike. "Between you and me I know you run things around here, keep everything shipshape, but I want you to keep an eye on Clay for me. He's got a lot on his plate with this wedding, and I can't afford to have things slipping here. Can I rely on you to let me know if there are any issues?"

He saw relief sweep Stanley's face, who nodded keenly and jumped up. "Of course I will, Mr Finch. You can rely on me."

Frankie might have imagined it, but he thought he saw a glint of triumph in Stanley's eye. He let out a slow breath. Stanley would probably love to be the one in charge instead of Clay.

He supposed it was only natural that there would be some inter-firm rivalry, and he was willing to bet that Clay didn't make shy, hardworking Stan's life particularly easy. But still, Frankie didn't need the aggro. *Why couldn't people just be happy with their lot in life? They were both earning good money, had good jobs.*

The last thing he needed on top of everything else was a power struggle brewing at the club.

Frankie's next stop was Ivy's house. He needed to find out why she'd left. Something about her leaving just didn't sit right with him.

"You stay in the car for this one Chris. She's more likely to be honest if it's just me. I don't want her feeling intimidated."

He rang the doorbell, and after a moment, the door was opened by Ivy's mum who looked delighted to see Frankie standing on her doorstep.

"Morning Mrs Pinner," he smiled. "You're looking as lovely as always today."

"Oh, Mr Finch," she giggled, patting her curls. "You are a charmer. Can I get you a cup of tea?"

"That would be just the ticket, I'm parched, thanks. I've come to see Ivy."

Frankie winced as Ivy's mum screeched up the stairs. "Ivy, get down here, you've got a visitor."

Fucking hell that woman had a pair of lungs on her.

"Go in the front room Mr Finch, and I'll bring your

cup of tea through."

Frankie sank into the floral sofa with its crocheted cushions, which was obviously saved for best and had rarely been sat on. The room was immaculate, but the air was stale, and he was willing to bet the family weren't usually allowed in here. The door would be kept firmly shut unless they had an important guest.

"Mr Finch?"

Frankie turned and was dismayed by Ivy's dishevelled appearance, but quickly hid his grimace behind a cheery smile.

"Sit down, Ivy; I wanted to talk to you."

Ivy sat nervously opposite him. She looked a state. Totally different to the carefree girl he'd seen night after night in the club. She was pale and thin and looked like she was drowning in oversized clothes. Her hair was lank and greasy, her natural colour showing by an inch at the roots in stark comparison to the harsh white blonde.

"How are you, Ivy? I only heard today you'd left the club."

She shrugged with a trace of defensiveness. "I'm OK, thanks."

"Don't take this the wrong way, but you don't look OK. Can you tell me what happened?"

She glanced at him with frightened eyes, and Frankie held up a hand in reassurance.

"You're not in trouble; I just want to know what happened."

Her brow creased, and she looked down at her hands. At that moment, her mum bustled into the room, holding a tray with a cup of tea and a large slice of cherry cake. She smiled indulgently at Frankie as she set it down on the coffee table in front of him. "Let me know if I can get you anything else, Mr Finch."

Ivy waited until her mum had left the room before speaking.

"There's not much to say. I was fired."

"When was this?"

"The night of the engagement party. I spilt those drinks and Clay told me to go."

"What else happened?"

She shrugged again. "Nothing, that's it."

"Did you spill the drinks on purpose?"

She looked up at him, horrified. "No! Of course not. Some guy put his hand up my skirt as I was about to put the drinks down, and it made me jump. I'd never do anything like that on purpose!"

"I believe you, Ivy. Linda mentioned she saw that. And what have you been doing since? Have you got another job?"

She shook her head, and Frankie groaned inwardly as he saw a tear run down her cheek.

For fuck's sake, he thought. He hated it when women cried.

"Is there something else going on Ivy?" he asked, wincing slightly and not sure he really wanted to know the answer. She let out a big sob, and Frankie tried not to roll his eyes. He should never have asked. He searched desperately around the room as Ivy sat there, now crying properly, her shoulders shaking as she stared down into her lap. He gratefully spotted a box of tissues and handed them to her.

"Thanks," she sniffed.

"Now, take your time. I want to know exactly what's been going on."

So Ivy told him the whole story about being pregnant. Once she started talking, she seemed unable to stop, regardless of her inappropriate audience and oblivious to the mortified look on Frankie's face. He sighed to himself. *So Clay had got Ivy pregnant, had he?*

She made him promise that he wouldn't say anything and, prepared to do anything at that point to avoid a fresh round of sobbing, Frankie agreed, but he felt growing anger towards Clay.

He pushed his piece of cake towards Ivy.

"If you're pregnant, you need to be looking after yourself. Eat this. You look like you haven't been eating properly."

Ivy picked a tiny morsel of cake and hovered it by her mouth before putting it back on the plate, tears welling in her eyes again. *Oh, for Christ's sake. What was the matter now?*

"Sorry, Mr Finch. It's the morning sickness, I've got it something terrible. I just don't seem to be able to keep anything down."

Now, this was something Frankie could offer advice on. Having been through two of Linda's pregnancies, he knew something about morning sickness, which Linda had suffered from until a health visitor had suggested eating ginger biscuits first thing in the morning. She'd taken to having a packet on the bedside table, and if she ate one while she was still horizontal, it had prevented the daily headlong rush to throw up, which had been an unpleasant way to start the day for both of them.

Ivy didn't want to be rude but was clearly sceptical about Frankie's advice.

"Trust me," he said, glad to be back on firmer ground. "It got Linda through two pregnancies and nipped her morning sickness in the bud. Go on, eat. You look like you need to get some food inside you."

Ivy nodded and slowly chewed on a small piece of cake, terrified she'd suddenly feel the need to throw up. Frankie patiently sat and watched her until half the cake had gone.

"Does your mum know?"

She shook her head, tears pooling again.

Frankie hastily stood. "Shall I have a word with her? Break the news? And get her to go easy on you. You need someone looking after you right now."

She nodded reluctantly, and Frankie made a swift and grateful exit.

Mrs Pinner wasn't too surprised by Frankie's announcement. Or if she was, she hid it well. She told him she suspected that might be the case, but Ivy had been refusing to talk to her. At least she now knew for sure.

"That boy's never been able to keep it in his trousers, and Ivy's always been too sweet on him."

"And you're not to go talking to him about it now. She doesn't want him to know, especially with him getting married."

"He's what? Oh, no wonder she's been in such a state. She needs to find herself a decent young man. Someone who's going to look after her, not a dog with two dicks like Clarence Caulder." She shook her head in irritation. "Is she going to keep it?"

Frankie's eyes widened. That was definitely outside his remit. "I have no idea Mrs Pinner, I think that's a conversation for the two of you. All I know is she needs some looking after. She's been left in the lurch, she's frightened, and she's feeling poorly, so I don't want to hear that you've been tearing strips off her."

"As if I would Mr Finch," she said in indignation and Frankie chuckled to himself. She offered him another cup of tea, but he'd had more than enough of sorting out women's problems today. He needed to get out of here.

On his way out, he stuck his head back into the front room and was pleased to see the plate was empty. He gave Ivy a thumbs-up, and she threw him a grateful smile.

"How would you feel about working in the chip shop for me? It's not as exciting as working in the club, but it's regular hours, and you could have the day shift, which I'm guessing might suit you better right now."

"Really?"

"Of course, really. I don't talk for the sake of it. Unlike some," he added under his breath, thinking of Ivy's mum.

"That would be great, thank you."

"Right then," he said, looking her up and down. The job's yours on two conditions. One is that you start looking after yourself and eat properly." She nodded gravely, "and the second is that you go and get your hair sorted out. You had beautiful hair before, and I'm guessing since you lost your job you haven't been able to afford to sort it out."

Ivy reddened and tucked a strand of unwashed hair behind her ear.

Frankie peeled a couple of £50 notes off a roll in his pocket and handed them to her. "Have a talk with your mum, then get yourself down to the hairdressers in the morning and get yourself sorted out. Stop trying to be someone you're not; you're just right as you are. And don't let one man's poor judgement convince you otherwise. Understand?" She nodded again. "Then get yourself to The Codfather for 11am tomorrow. Can you do that?"

She nodded again, then as Frankie was turning to leave, she launched herself at him, enveloping him in a tight hug.

"Thank you," she whispered and gave him a kiss on the cheek.

Frankie didn't blush, he wasn't that sort of man, but he could feel bloody uncomfortable, and he did now. He waited till she released him then strode quickly to the door.

"Remember Ivy: Food, haircut and be at work at 11 tomorrow."

And he swiftly left while he still had some dignity.

He climbed back into the car with a sense of relief. "Give me the Albanian mob any day compared to this," he said.

24
THE HAPPY COUPLE

Pandora beamed as she and Clay emerged onto the steps of the registry office. She gazed lovingly at her new husband as they stood to have their photo taken and slipped her hand into his, the wedding ring feeling unfamiliar on her finger.

The wedding had been a small affair, just the two of them plus Frankie as best man, Bea as maid of honour and Clay's mum. It was an icy-cold winter's day, but Pandora glowed with such joy that she didn't feel the cold despite her outfit.

She'd made a concession to it being a winter wedding by covering up a little more flesh than usual, but she wasn't exactly wrapped up. The dress was long-sleeved with fine, translucent French lace on the bodice and sleeves, and dipped down to practically nothing at the back, leaving a lot of exposed skin for such a cold day. Clay hugged her close while the photographer arranged her big tulle skirt for the photographs.

This was it; they'd done it! They were married! It had been a simple ceremony, but that hadn't detracted from the beauty of it. Neither of them wanted a big fuss over the wedding itself. Besides, they were more than making up for that with the reception afterwards.

So far, the day had gone without any problems. The only fly in the ointment had been when they signed the register and Clay had murmured with a proud smile that she was Mrs Caulder now. Pandora had given a little laugh. "Oh come on," she whispered in response to his questioning look, "there's no way I'm becoming Pandora Caulder, no matter how much I love you. I need to keep my stage name!"

In hindsight perhaps she should have mentioned that before the wedding, but it would only have caused a row. And after all, she'd never actually agreed she'd take his name.

"I'm your wife now, that's what matters." And she'd shushed his protestations with a lingering kiss. And because he was the happiest man in the world at that moment, he'd accepted that.

A classic white Daimler was idling at the curb for them, and as soon as the photographer released them, they dashed for the back of it, clutching each other and relishing the warmth.

Frankie, Bea and Clay's mum would make their own way to the club. Pandora couldn't think of a less comfortable group of people and giggled to herself as she imagined the forced conversations they'd have on the ride to the reception. She wished she could be a fly on the wall.

Finally, alone they looked at each other, both grinning.

"Hello, wife," said Clay.

"Hello, husband" smiled Pandora as she leaned into him. As their lips met their smiles were replaced with the familiar heat that always lingered just below the surface.

The chauffeur looked back at them, clutched in their embrace, and smiled wistfully. He'd seen that elation and adoration countless times. *Newlyweds,* he thought, shaking his head ruefully. *I wonder how long that'll last.*

25
A NEW BEGINNING

The chauffeur pulled up outside the club and wondered whether he should interrupt the couple in the back. He'd give them a minute or two. After all, you get precious little time to yourselves on your wedding day. As soon as they were out of the car, they'd be the centre of attention, busy with friends and family for the rest of the day.

He stole another glance. *They didn't look like they'd be resurfacing any time soon.*

They all jumped at a loud rap on the window. Pandora and Clay pulled reluctantly apart. Angie, dressed in her habitual black despite the occasion, jerked her thumb towards the entrance. They needed to get inside. Pandora unclipped her little handbag and quickly retouched her lipstick while the chauffeur came round to open the door for her. She emerged in a cloud of tulle skirt which they all helped her to get under control. She threw the chauffeur a grateful smile and took Clay's hand.

"Come on, husband, let's do this!"

Stanley had outdone himself, under strict instruction from Angie of course, who had planned the whole event meticulously and with military precision. The club looked spectacular. With daylight rapidly fading the space was lit with a thousand tiny lights. They wound up the palm trees and were strung across the overhanging glass canopy that covered part of the terrace and protected the guests from the worst of the English weather.

Pandora gasped, it looked magical. Everyone stood and applauded as they entered the room, and they both grinned, neither able to shake the gleeful expressions from their faces.

The photographer had arrived ahead of them and was busy snapping away, so they paused on the threshold for yet more pictures.

Initially, Pandora hadn't been sold on a winter wedding, but this was amazing. And besides, neither of them had wanted to wait another six months. They were both impatient to get married, Pandora not least because Angie kept reminding her she needed to get back in the papers before she was completely forgotten.

She felt a pang of sadness that her parents weren't here and wondered for the millionth time whether she should have invited them. No, she refused to think about them today. She wouldn't let them spoil her special day. They never approved of anything she did, and they certainly wouldn't approve of Clay. Instead, the club was filled with well-wishers, from people she'd worked with on the film to celebrities and friends of Clay's from the club. She was determined that today would be the best day of her life.

"I can't wait to get you on your own," Clay murmured in her ear as they posed for photos, and her grin widened further.

They were having a champagne reception, followed by a sit-down meal, but they should be able to sneak off while she changed for the evening party. Pandora felt like a princess in her big floaty skirt, but it was no good for dancing in, and as Angie had pointed out, the more outfits she wore, the more photos would get into the papers.

All the same, it felt like an age until they finally got some time to themselves, by which time they were both desperate to be alone. Pandora ran her hand up Clay's thigh while Frankie was giving his speech, and he turned to her, the yearning visible on his face.

"Soon," she mouthed.

As soon as the speeches were over, the lights dimmed, and the band started playing. They'd both decided to skip having a first dance. They had a dance of a different kind in mind, and the big fairytale skirt was getting on Pandora's nerves.

As they slipped away to the office hand in hand, they giggled together. *Today had been such an adventure.*

Closing the office door behind them, Pandora pressed herself against Clay, the mountain of tulle getting between them, making the office feel a lot smaller than usual. She gave an exasperated huff and stepped backwards, reaching behind her to unclip the large skirt which fell away, revealing a skin-tight lace dress which had been underneath the whole time. The delicate lace from the bodice extended down to the tops of her thighs then there was a large translucent panel before the lace crept in again towards the bottom of the dress. She bundled up the huge pile of tulle and threw it over the other side of the desk then stood, arms outstretched. "So, what do you think?"

Clay shook his head. *He hadn't expected that. Wow, she looked magic. He didn't think she could top the first dress, but this was even sexier.* She looked up at him from underneath her lashes and backed towards the desk, wriggling the skirt upwards as she went until it was up around her waist.

Clay's breath caught as he watched her. Seeing the heat in his eyes, she beckoned, then put a hand against his chest to stop him briefly. "I've had too many wardrobe malfunctions here already, and there's no way I'm getting out of this dress easily, so no ripping it, OK? I need to wear this for the rest of the evening."

Clay growled as he quickly closed the gap between them, shrugging his jacket onto the floor.

And then they both forgot everything other than the heat, desire and urgency that they were both so addicted to.

26
NOT THE BEST START

The next morning Clay woke first and lay for a moment just looking at his wife. Her face looked angelic in repose, her hair tousled and wild. He smiled. Even asleep, she was beautiful. He truly was the luckiest man alive.

He edged the covers down slightly to expose her breasts, her nipples instantly hardening in response. She stirred and he took her nipple into his mouth and gently sucked, being rewarded by a soft moan.

A smile played on her lips as she woke and began to move and respond. They weren't having a honeymoon, but Frankie had booked them the honeymoon suite at the Dorchester, and they planned to make the most of it. Two days in bed with room service and no obligations. Bliss.

Sometime later, they lay in bed, Pandora with a croissant in one hand while Clay tucked into a large cooked breakfast. Newspapers were spread all around them, and Pandora leafed through as she ate.

She was delighted. They were on the front pages of most of the papers, except the Guardian who'd gone with a headline about some Tory MP taking backhanders, but even there they'd made it onto page two.

The Starlet and the Gangster, shouted The Sun, running a picture of them kissing on the steps, Clay's scar red and visible. Pandora pored over the papers, while Clay tucked into breakfast. He had no interest in the press; he was starving.

Pandora slipped off to the bathroom while Clay finished his eating, and when she returned, she was wearing a short white silk slip. Clay immediately forgot about the remaining food on his plate, his eyes wide. She padded slowly towards him.

"Wow," he breathed.

"You like it?"

He nodded.

"I was going to wear it last night, but well, we were in a bit of a hurry as I remember. I thought it would be a shame to let it go to waste."

Clay nodded again. He didn't know what to say; she looked, wow.

She moved towards him, slipping the satin straps off her shoulders and letting the slip fall to the floor, revealing tiny, translucent barely-there white underwear. It was breathtakingly sexy. There wasn't much of it, but she looked sensational. It didn't really hide anything; instead it just kind of framed all the bits Clay was interested in with pretty little scraps of ribbon and lace.

Clay quickly put the tray of room service on the floor, and she pulled the bed covers away. He was already at full attention, and she smiled as she straddled him, kissing his chest, then his stomach, teasing and tormenting him until she relented, taking him into her mouth.

He lay back against the pillows watching her before his eyes closed and his head rocked back. A phone rang, but they both ignored it. After all, they were only newlyweds once. Everything else could wait.

Afterwards, they lay in bed, flushed and grinning, their

breath slowly returning to normal. Pandora reached over to get her phone.

"Who was it?"

"Angie."

Clay scrunched up his face.

"Don't call her back," he complained and attempted to grab the phone. "We've only got one more day as our honeymoon, let's make the most of it."

She laughed and scooted out of his grasp, wrapping a sheet around herself and walking into the next room. She dialled her agent.

"How are my newlyweds this morning?"

Pandora beamed.

'Wonderful, thank you. I could totally get used to this."

"Well, I hate to interrupt your love-in honey, but I've got an opportunity that's too big to pass up. Barclay Soames is in town auditioning for his new movie. He's seen your photos in the paper this morning and got straight on the phone. He wants you to go and audition."

"Oh my God, really?" Barclay Soames was one of Hollywood's biggest directors. And he was asking to see Pandora?

"Yes, and don't worry. There's no casting couch this time honey, but if you don't want to miss out, you need to get yourself down to the Palace Theatre pronto. He flies out this evening, so if you don't get down there ASAP, you'll miss your chance."

Pandora looked through to the bedroom where Clay was propped up on one elbow watching her. She felt a pang of guilt, but she couldn't miss this opportunity. Clay would understand. He'd have to.

As it turned out, Clay didn't understand. In fact, he couldn't believe she wanted to dash off for some job interview instead of staying with him in the honeymoon suite.

He slid his arms around her waist as she stood putting

her makeup on, kissing her neck in an attempt to lure her back to bed, but she just laughed and shooed him away.

By the time she emerged from the bathroom, he was back in bed sulking.

Pandora sat down next to him and put a hand on his cheek. Covering his scar, she wondered whether he would be even more handsome without it. Or was it the juxtaposition that made him so attractive? She couldn't decide.

"I'm sorry to dash off darling, but this is a once-in-a-lifetime opportunity that I just can't pass up. You know how thin on the ground work has been recently, I can't miss this chance."

Clay snorted. "Our honeymoon only happens once too. I'd have thought that was more important. I can only imagine how pleased you'd be if Frankie called me to go do something for him today."

"I'd understand," she said. But as the words left her mouth, she wasn't sure they were true. "Anyway," she added, "I won't be long. You stay here, order room service, chill out and catch up on your sleep, so you've got plenty of strength by the time I get back." She wiggled her eyebrows and ran her hand down his chest, almost getting distracted by his naked body again. The corner of his mouth twitched.

"Are you sure you want to go?" he said, pulling her towards him on the bed.

She sank into him for a moment then pushed away, straightening her skirt.

"Back soon," she promised and dashed out of the room before he could change her mind.

Clay sank back against the pillows and blew out a fed-up sigh. Well, this wasn't how he'd imagined his honeymoon. It was great to see her so excited about this interview, but it made him uneasy. They were married now. And even though they hadn't discussed it, he'd assumed her priorities would change.

Although perhaps it was only natural that would take a bit of time. She'd been so ambitious for so many years it would take a while to adjust to being married and settling down.

Still, she wouldn't be gone more than a couple of hours, and he had plans for her return. With that thought, he let his eyes close and drifted into a deep sleep.

But by the time Clay woke, it was getting dark, and there was no sign of Pandora. He pulled on a robe and went to stand on the balcony. The lights of London were twinkling, and the city looked magical in all its Christmassy splendour. Which made him feel all the more sour that Pandora wasn't here to share this with him.

He tried calling her, but she didn't pick up. He could call Angie and see if she'd heard anything, but what was the point? Besides, he didn't want to sound desperate, asking where his wife was while they were supposed to be honeymooning. So instead, he showered, dressed and went down to the bar. There was no point hanging out in the honeymoon suite by himself. He left a scribbled message for Pandora in the room. She could come and find him when she finally got back.

But Pandora didn't come back, and so Clay kept on drinking. The beautiful surroundings did nothing to improve his mood. The place was great, but the high-end bar with its polished mahogany furniture and piano player wasn't somewhere he'd choose to drink. He was only here because it was his fucking honeymoon. So why was he alone?

It was gone nine by the time Pandora walked into the bar, looking thrilled. Her smile faded as she was faced by a drunk and angry Clay.

"Oh look, it's my wife," he said to the barman, voice dripping with sarcasm. The barman discreetly found something else to do. He turned to Pandora. "I'd nearly forgotten what you looked like you've been gone so long."

"Haha, funny," she said. "Sorry it took longer than I expected, but it went really well. He said he'd be in touch in the next couple of days to confirm, but it sounds like I've got the job."

Clay shrugged. He didn't care. "Great. That makes me feel a lot better that I spent our honeymoon by myself."

"Hey, I wasn't gone that long!" she said, keeping a lid on her anger and trying to placate Clay, "and besides," she said running her hand up his chest, "I'm back now. Come on; we've only got this amazing suite for another night. Let's make the most of it."

He turned away."Maybe I'm enjoying myself here now."

She raised an eyebrow, exasperated. He was acting like a petulant child. Had he been drinking for the whole time she'd been gone?

"Right, well I'm going up to our room. You can join me if you want to."

Clay watched her leave and then turned his stare back to his empty glass. He clicked his fingers at the barman. "Fill her up."

27
TAKING CARE OF BUSINESS

Frankie rubbed Linda's shoulders, his fingers working the tension away before leaning into her and whispering something suggestive into her ear. She squeaked in surprise.

"Frankie Finch you do pick your moments," she laughed, threatening him with a wooden spoon dripping with the bolognese sauce she was stirring. He backed away, smiling, hands raised in surrender and went to the fridge to grab himself a drink.

Linda's mother was on her way over for dinner, so he knew his chances were slim, but he liked the idea of trying to slip in a quicky while they waited for the doorbell to ring. After all, he thrived on danger. Still, with the kids and Chris in the next room and Linda's mum due any second that was probably a step too far. He slid his arms back around Linda and nuzzled her neck.

His phone buzzed. Pulling it out of his pocket, he touched the screen, and immediately his mood changed from playful to deadly serious.

"What?" said Linda, sensing the shift.

He planted a brisk kiss on her cheek. "I need to go out. Can you do something for me? It's important." Linda raised an eyebrow, but Frankie ignored it.

"Get your mum to look after little Ronnie; you know how she loves having time with the baby so she won't complain. Then get Chris to take you and Britney to the cinema. You said she's been going on about seeing that new Disney movie, so make a girls' night out of it. And I want to hear all about it when I get back."

"And you're going where while we have this sudden girl's night out?"

"You don't need to worry about that. I've got some business to attend to. Won't be long."

"But," he added in an undertone, "you need to make sure Chris goes into the cinema with you, okay? I don't care if he doesn't want to see the film. No excuses."

Linda reluctantly agreed. She almost demanded to know what was going on but thought better of it. It sounded suspiciously like she was giving Chris an alibi. Perhaps she didn't want to know why.

Just then, the doorbell rang, and Linda smoothed her dress with a sigh. Her mum was expecting a family dinner, not to be stuck babysitting, so she wasn't relishing this conversation. Then again, Frankie was right; she was such a proud grandma; she wouldn't mind some quality time alone with her new grandson.

Fluffing her hair, she threw Frankie an unimpressed look and went to open the front door. Frankie made a swift exit before his mother-in-law could spot him and, pulling a second phone out of his pocket, he dialled Sem the crem. It was time to call in that favour.

28
SCRAMBLED EGGS & CHAMPAGNE

Clay scowled as he pulled the door closed behind him. It was nearly six, and his stomach grumbled, reminding him he hadn't eaten today. He'd hoped Pandora would get home before he had to leave for work, but it looked like he would miss her, again. She'd been up and out this morning while he was still out cold from the night before, an occupational hazard of working in a nightclub.

After the wedding, they'd moved into Clay's flat together and had done their best to smooth things over, but things weren't back to normal after the disastrous honeymoon. Clay felt Pandora had really let him down by choosing the audition over him, and she was still peeved by his behaviour. After all, she'd come straight to find him and share her good news only to find him drunk and bad-tempered. By the time he had finally made it back from the bar that night, he could hardly walk straight, and Pandora was already asleep or pretending to be. He'd fallen into bed fully dressed, reeking of whiskey and they slept with their backs turned to one another.

They both felt bruised by the experience, aggrieved but

reluctant to start another argument. Pandora was shooting a fragrance campaign and had been up and out early every morning this week. That irritated him. She knew he worked nights, and he suspected she was avoiding him to punish him for some reason. He knew he could talk her round, but only if he actually saw her.

Clay felt a pang of sadness as he reached the club, and paused by the curb for a moment remembering how happy they were arriving here on their wedding day. It was hard to believe that it was only a week ago.

Perhaps he should make an effort, do something nice for her. It was Saturday tomorrow, so they'd be at home together during the day. He'd take her out somewhere nice for lunch, and they could spend the rest of the day in bed. That was what they needed. Then everything would go back to normal.

But the next morning Pandora got a jump start on him. She'd had a similar idea, and he woke up to a tray of home-cooked breakfast in bed, with Buck's Fizz and scrambled eggs. Pandora wasn't a natural cook, she'd never had much interest in food, and the scrambled eggs were rubbery and slightly grey. But Clay didn't care. *This was more like it.* She was clearly making an effort, and he was sure her cooking would improve with practice.

He choked down the last of the scrambled egg and washed it down with the Buck's Fizz. He would have preferred a cup of tea.

She perched on the side of the bed, watching him.

"So, how was my celebration breakfast then?"

"It was a lovely thought..." he said. Then seeing her wince, he added, "No, really!"

"Don't tell me, the eggs were awful."

"Well yes," his face broke into a sheepish smile. "But I'm sure with practice..."

"Oy," she said, laughing and hitting him with a pillow. He grabbed her wrists and pulled her in towards him, kissing her slowly, then making her gasp as he rolled them over, so he was on top, looking down at her. Their kissing deepened. Her satin dressing gown was the only thing between them, and that soon found its way to the floor.

They both felt better afterwards, lying amongst the rumpled sheets, flushed and relieved that things were back to some kind of normal. Whatever their differences, sex was something that they did very well.

"Your talents definitely lie in the bedroom rather than the kitchen," chuckled Clay.

Pandora play-slapped him but refused to get annoyed by the comment. He was probably right, even if it did make her sound a bit like a whore. Besides, nothing could spoil her mood today.

She ran a finger down his chest.

"Anyway, aren't you going to ask me what we're celebrating?"

"Oh yeah, celebration breakfast, wasn't it? I thought we were just celebrating the weekend."

"No, silly! I got the part!" She squealed, sitting up and leaning over him. Clay was distracted by her breasts now being inches away from his face. He ran a hand over one of them.

"You're looking at the lead actress in the new Barclay Soames movie!"

"That's great sweetheart," said Clay, hand sliding down her back and pulling her in towards him. He'd hardly seen her all week, and he was ready for round two. But she wasn't going to be sidetracked.

"It's being filmed at Pinewood Studios, which is so convenient. It could really be the start of something big. Soames is huge in Hollywood, and if this movie comes off, it could be my ticket to the big time."

Clay's hands had reached the curve of her back, his mouth now tracing kisses along her collarbone. "That's amazing", he murmured, rolling back on top of her and claiming her mouth with his. With her hair all mussed and face pink, she looked wonderful. He didn't care whether she was a big star or not; he wanted her all to himself.

Her body responded to his, and she moved against him.

What was it with this woman, she made him insatiable!

He paused, pulling away for a moment.

"Hey, I was thinking about something too. How would you feel about starting a family?"

Pandora wrinkled her nose and snorted. "No thanks! What famous actress can you name that had kids at this stage of their career? I'm not ruining this figure until I've well and truly made it thank you very much!" Then spotting the hurt look in Clay's eyes, she relented. "I'm not saying never, just in a few years, that's all."

He looked slightly mollified, but still unhappy, and she gave a small sigh. Perhaps this is something they should have discussed before getting married. She ran her fingers lightly along his sides, making him wriggle, and fixed him with those big eyes, heavy-lidded with desire. She murmured, "Besides we can have great fun practising in the meantime. After all, they say having kids ruins your sex life, don't they? There would be no spending the day doing this…" she shoved him onto his back and straddled him, "so I say let's make the most of it." And as her hips began to move any other thoughts were driven out of his head as he once again succumbed to this woman and the strength of the chemistry between them.

29
COPPERS & CAKE

No matter how confident you are, finding two uniformed policemen on the doorstep can give the toughest of men a frisson of anxiety.

"Could we come in, Mr Finch?'

After a split second of hesitation, Frankie's habitual charm kicked in. There were people in life that were worth needlessly antagonising, and people who weren't. The police fell firmly into the second category. "Of course officers, can I get you some coffee?" he said, leading them through to the kitchen.

"No, thank you, Mr Finch, not while we're on duty," said the taller, rather officious young man, and Frankie had to stop himself from rolling his eyes.

Linda, who had just settled baby Ronnie off to sleep, walked in and on seeing their guests immediately took command of the situation, making them sit down and putting a plate of cake in front of each of them. "I know how hard you boys work, out on the streets all day. I bet you haven't even had a proper breakfast yet."

"Well no, we haven't actually Mrs Finch. Not since

coming on shift at 5.30 this morning. My tummy's been rumbling something terrible," said the shorter of the two.

She gave him an indulgent smile, before throwing an eyes-narrowed glance at Frankie over her shoulder as she went to put the kettle on.

The taller police officer steadfastly ignored his cake and took the lead. "That's very kind of you, Mrs Finch, but we're here looking for Chris Slaughter. He resides at this address, is that correct?"

Frankie looked up. "Have you got news about his mum's murder then?"

"We can't discuss an ongoing investigation Mr Finch", said the smaller man, his tone of authority slightly undermined by a mouthful of chocolate cake. Frankie raised an eyebrow but bit back his response.

"I'll get him for you."

Chris appeared a few minutes later, looking drawn and anxious. The policemen, who now had steaming cups of tea in front of them, got to their feet, all business once again.

"Any news? Have you made an arrest?"

"I'm afraid not Mr Slaughter; we're here about a different matter. We've had a report of a missing person, and we're following up on that."

Chris frowned. The taller policeman pulled a notebook from his pocket.

"We're trying to trace the whereabouts of a Mr Nico Ymeri, also known as Nick.

Chris's eyes narrowed, and his hands balled into fists.

"Are you serious?"

"We understand he's a suspect in your mother's murder, but he's been reported as missing. Have you seen him recently?"

Chris's mouth compressed into a tight line. "Not for weeks."

"Where were you two nights ago, Mr Slaughter?"

"Are you kidding me? That kid has been going around

boasting to everyone who'll listen that he stabbed my mum, a sick old lady. And instead of going after him, you're questioning me?"

"We're obliged to follow up on anyone reported missing. I'm sure you understand."

Chris was about to respond that *no, he fucking didn't understand* when Frankie put a hand on his shoulder.

"Just answer the question."

Chris made a visible effort to calm down while he racked his brain for what he'd been doing that night. "I was at the cinema."

"And where was that?"

Chris's eyes narrowed, his anger returning. Why were they questioning him about this?

"Has something happened to him?"

"We're just investigating a missing person's report, Mr Slaughter. Answer the question please."

"I was at the Isleworth Multiplex."

"And which film did you see?"

Chris rolled his eyes and pulled out his wallet, finding a folded cinema ticket and handing it over.

The tall policeman's mouth tugged at the corner before he regained his composure. He gave Chris a sceptical look.

"You don't look like a *Rainbow Princess 3* kind of guy if I'm honest."

"I went with Mrs Finch and her daughter," he said reddening.

The policeman nodded, smiling to himself.

"Okay, thanks for that. We needed to ask. I'll be in touch if we have any more questions."

"Lovely cup of tea Mrs Finch, thanks."

Frankie closed the door behind them and walked back to the kitchen.

Chris gave him a searching look and murmured, "Was that what I think it was?"

"Let's put it this way," said Frankie. "I don't think he'll

be showing up any time soon."

30
BUTTERFLIES & BLUSHES

After a restless night, Pandora felt drained and anxious. Today was the first day on set shooting the Barclay Soames *Lancelot* movie. She still couldn't believe she'd been cast as Guinevere opposite king of Hollywood rom-coms Henri Deveraux. He, of course, was taking the title role, but despite the cast having been running their lines for a fortnight, he hadn't yet made an appearance.

Barclay waved this off, saying Henri was busy doing publicity for another project. He didn't seem concerned, so why should she be? Still, it felt strange that she hadn't even met her co-star. She had to admit to feeling nervous about coming face to face with someone so famous.

The past few weeks had been fun, although far from glamorous. She and the other actors had been meeting in a rehearsal room in Camden to run through the script. Pandora had arrived on the first day of rehearsals glammed up to the max in a dress and heels, but after a day of freezing her arse off, she realised practical was the way to go. By the end of the week, she was wearing jeans and a big jumper, not to mention a hat and scarf at the start of each day before the heating kicked in.

Barclay, who wanted to be involved in every aspect of the movie, was there directing rehearsals. He was a difficult man, demanding and a perfectionist, but the childish delight he showed when he found the magic he was looking for made it all worthwhile. Pandora gradually came to realise why he was one of the best directors in the business.

Over those weeks they'd all bonded as a group, going for lunch together and working late into the evenings to get ready for filming to start, and she felt like she'd found a new family. She wondered how a big star like Henri stepping in would change the dynamic.

Walking into the film studios, everything suddenly felt different. Pandora had seen her costume for the first time today, and it sank home just how different a role this was for her. The dress she'd be wearing today was a beautifully embroidered long robe which would sweep the floor when she walked, and her trademark platinum hair would be covered with a long strawberry-blonde wig. She could almost do with a day just to acclimatise to looking and feeling so different, but as Barclay constantly pointed out: Time was money, and they were on a tight schedule. They had no scope for endless takes. She felt a frisson of nerves in her stomach. No amount of cleavage or sultry pouting would get her out of a jam in this production. This was a job for a real actress.

Pandora sat in the makeup chair while a girl, who introduced herself as Toni and who had garish pink hair and countless facial piercings, spent an hour giving her a totally natural look. Gone were her habitual dark lashes and eyeliner, and there wasn't red lip in sight. She pushed down a rising panic as she realised just how different she was going to look. Was this the right thing to do? She'd put a lot of time and effort into creating a bombshell image. Would this damage that? Would she be a laughing stock? She assessed herself in the mirror. She looked natural, albeit in a way that emphasised her beauty, not in a way that showed the dark circles under her eyes or the spot threatening on her forehead. And thankfully Toni had expertly covered up the mark Clay had left on her neck. Pandora felt a flash of irritation as she thought back to that night, annoyed with herself that she hadn't noticed him sucking on the side of her neck until it was too late, but to be fair, they were in the throes of passion at the time. She wasn't sure whether he'd done it just to annoy her, or whether he'd wanted it to be some kind of brand of ownership. Either way, she had been furious with him. They weren't teenagers for fuck's sake!

She twisted her wedding ring for a moment, then removed it, placing it down in front of the mirror. After all, she couldn't wear that for filming.

Makeup done, Toni started pinning Pandora's hair back and covering it in a fine net ready for the wig. Pandora closed her eyes and ran her lines through in her head. She knew the scene inside out but was still starting to get butterflies. As the least experienced, she didn't want to mess this up. She took a deep breath, trying to calm her nerves.

Toni gave a surprised gasp, and Pandora's eyes flicked open and immediately saw why. Henri Devereau, in full swashbuckling Lancelot costume, had just walked in. *Of course, he'd picked this moment to come in*, when she had her hair scraped back in an unflattering nylon skull cap and looked like she was bald. *Awesome*. Oh, and she looked barefaced and was wearing a dressing gown.

He smiled, his tan crinkling around his eyes.

"Enchanté, Mademoiselle Pandora," he murmured, bending to kiss her hand as if she was the most beautiful creature he'd ever seen. Despite her mortification, Pandora felt a flutter in her stomach. She could see why he was still an onscreen heartthrob after fifteen years in the business. The man oozed charm; it wasn't all just onscreen magic.

"I just wished to say a brief hello before we meet on set, à bientôt."

He gave a little bow and left. Pandora and Toni exchanged wide-eyed glances and grinned. Pandora shook her head. Why did she have to meet him when she was at her least attractive? Oh well, this was a professional relationship, it's not like she wanted to get him into bed. Still, it would have been nice to make a better first impression.

The transformation from Pandora into Guinevere took a further half an hour, and once it was complete, she hardly recognised herself. Gone was the white-blonde hair replaced by much darker long waves and a natural face which made her look both younger and more serious. Inspecting her reflection, Pandora felt for the first time that perhaps she could pull this off, show the critics that she was more than just a piece of onscreen decoration or a gratuitous pair of tits.

There was a knock, and a breathless runner stuck his head around the door. "We're ready for you on set Ms Caine."

Toni squeezed her shoulder with a reassuring smile, and taking a deep breath Pandora walked onto the set.

31
IT'S BEEN EMOTIONAL

Frankie and Chris were tucking into pie and chips in The Codfather when the woman walked in.

Frankie, who habitually sat facing the door, eyed her and paused, a forkful of gravy-covered chips halfway to his mouth.

The woman looked like shit. She was probably in her early forties but wasn't wearing it well. Her eyes were puffy and sore, and she exuded a wired kind of desperation. Her eyes fixed onto Frankie like a lifeline, and she approached.

"Mr Finch. I'm sorry to bother you having your lunch and all, but I didn't know how else to find you. I need your help. It's my boy. He's missing and the police, they just don't seem to want to help." She paused and gulped down a sob, her hands twisting the scuffed plastic handbag she was clutching. "I tried coming to the club, but they wouldn't let me in."

Thank fuck for that, thought Frankie. *She would have scared off the punters.*

"And what makes you think I can help?"

The woman shrugged, her body slumping in despair. "I

don't know who else to turn to. And you know everything that goes on around here. My boy, he's a good boy, but he's got in with some bad people, and I'm worried. I'm going mad with worry Mr Finch."

Frankie considered for a moment. The woman's eyes darted nervously around, continually searching for her missing son. Her nerves were clearly in shreds. Then her eyes landed on Chris, and she took a frightened step backwards.

He looked up at her, his face blank, and nodded in acknowledgement. "Mrs Ymeri."

The woman backed away.

"I..." she stammered. "I didn't know you two..."

Frankie put two and two together. This must be the mother of the boy who'd killed Chris's mum.

"Ah, Mrs Ymeri. I've heard about your boy. Nico isn't it?"

She froze, a tear dribbling unheeded from her nose, suddenly terrified of what Frankie would say next. She needed to know what had happened, but suddenly fear had turned into a horrible certainty.

"I heard he'd got himself mixed up with that Albanian gang," said Frankie, shaking his head. "Stupid boy. I hear they're pretty ruthless. If he's disappeared and you're wondering why I suggest you talk to them." The woman frowned, and Frankie continued. "Mind you; I wouldn't recommend it. Leave it to the police; I'm sure they're doing everything they can to find him. I take it they know who he was working for?"

The woman gave a small nod. Lack of sleep and desperation had taken their toll, and her brain felt fogged. She didn't know whether to believe Frankie or not. She knew Nico had got in with a bad crowd; she'd begged him to get himself a proper job and not get into trouble. But what she hadn't known was that Chris worked for Frankie Finch. That brought up a whole lot of new questions about his disappearance.

It was a small estate, and she'd heard the rumours about Nico being the one who stabbed Chris's mum. She didn't believe them; she couldn't believe her boy would do anything like that. But Chris knew Frankie, and if Frankie Finch believed it, that was all that mattered.

Unable to hold back the torrent of emotion any longer, she gave a keening wail and fled.

32
A NEW EXPERIENCE

Filming was going well. The cast and crew were getting on without any hissy fits or falling outs, and they were rattling through the production schedule. Barclay was delighted with progress. He'd done the right thing giving the role to Pandora. He'd had a niggling doubt that she might not be able to carry off a serious role, after all, she was untested in that capacity, but he'd seen her potential and decided to give her a chance.

A consummate workaholic, Barclay only slept for a few hours each night. As he waited for filming to start, he often found himself pacing his rented apartment in the early hours worrying that Pandora would turn his precious film into a kind of *Carry On Camelot*. But his fears had been unfounded. She'd stepped up and done a great job so far.

But today would be the real test. They were shooting the big seduction scene, where Guinevere finally succumbs to Lancelot. So far the chemistry had been good between Pandora and Henri, but it had been limited to loaded glances and a few tender moments. They hadn't so much as kissed yet, let alone had to do something as intimate as this. He just hoped they would make convincing onscreen lovers or the whole movie could flop.

Pandora was apprehensive. Of course, she was. She'd never filmed a sex scene before, and the thought of it was terrifying. Barclay had assured her that it would be a closed set and nothing to worry about, but that did little to calm her nerves.

It didn't help that she couldn't talk to Clay about any of this. She didn't think he'd handle the idea of her being naked in bed with another man. He'd probably go mental, or worse still insist on being on set, and she wasn't having that.

Pandora knew the scene inside out. She'd learned the script months ago, and they'd had a clothes-on rehearsal yesterday, which had been rather bizarre. It turned out a love scene in a movie was the least sexy thing in the world, more akin to choreographing a sweaty fight scene than anything romantic.

She'd so nearly laughed yesterday when they were rehearsing the blow by blow seduction with Barclay shouting out "Less thrusting people, we're not making a porno," and a running commentary of instructions. "Now Henri, slide your hand down her back and roll her over, so you are on top. 'Dora, try wrapping your legs around him while he kisses your neck. No, scrap that, you look like a sloth. Try legs on the bed please."

If she hadn't been so terrified by the thought of doing it for real, it would have been hilarious.

When she'd signed her contract, she'd agreed to a nudity clause stipulating she go topless in the movie, if the script warranted it. She hadn't minded, she wanted the film to be as good as it could be and it seemed silly to make a fuss after baring nearly everything in that calendar. It was only now as she sat in makeup that the realities of it were sinking in. This wasn't just having a few photos taken, it was getting up close and personal with another man, and it being filmed for the world to see. Clay was going to pitch a fit.

Today she was getting to know Toni rather better than before, as she was dusted with body makeup and concealer to cover her star tattoos. Toni was currently taping on a kind of G string to cover her modesty (although even just a tiny bit of it). Pandora nearly told her not to bother, she'd almost rather be completely naked than messing about like this, but then she thought about being pressed up close and personal against Henri and kept her mouth shut. He'd be wearing what was laughingly known in the business as a cock sock to prevent too much contact but all the same, the whole thing made her cringe. She'd be glad when today was over. She just hoped they'd get it right first time and wouldn't need a second day of filming the scene.

"All done! And looking gorgeous!" Toni said, straightening and looking at Pandora with professional satisfaction. "Now you just need to plumb the depths of your acting talent to drum up some chemistry," she sniggered.

"What do you mean?" frowned Pandora. Did the girl think she wasn't up to the job of acting this?

"Well, you're not going to be getting much of a reaction from him are you honey, so it's all going to be down to the acting."

"Why do you say that?"

Toni looked at her, hands on hips. "Surely, you know?"

"Know what?"

"That he prefers his between-the-sheets action with less boobs and more dick honey. Surely you'd picked up on that? At least you don't need to worry about him trying anything on with you!"

Pandora's mouth formed a surprised Oh! She hadn't realised that Henri was gay. That was actually a huge relief. And should go some way to placate Clay once he found out about it. How strange that he kept that quiet, but perhaps he liked keeping his private life just that, private. And she could understand why. He had made his name playing heterosexual male leads in rom-coms so perhaps he was just protecting his career.

Toni smiled and pulled a small bottle of vodka from her handbag, offering it to Pandora.

"I thought you might need a bit of Dutch courage this morning. It's nerve-wracking for any actor to do a sex scene, let alone if it's their first one."

Pandora took a grateful swig, feeling the liquid warm her on its way down. She could do this.

Barclay eventually called it a wrap just after 6pm, much to everyone's relief. Simulating passion wasn't the fun it promised to be and soon became tiresome. Once she had overcome her initial embarrassment, they both just concentrated on getting the scene right. Being a closed set, it had felt a bit like a surreal ménage à trois between Pandora, Henri and Barclay. Only it was the unsexiest threesome imaginable. You got all the anxiety and fear of a first encounter with none of the pleasure to accompany it. Over and over for about eight hours.

Pandora found it hard to believe the filming would end up being convincing on the big screen, especially as they lay there being spritzed with rose water by Toni to simulate a sexy glow. There was so much that was added when it was all cut together, that was where the real magic happened. She just had to trust that Barclay knew what he was doing.

She felt relief flood her as she got dressed again. She'd done it. She'd got her first sex scene in the bag, and it hadn't been as mortifying as she thought. Barclay made it all seem so normal and business-like for her, made her feel comfortable. And Henri hadn't been bothered at all. Was that just because he was a man, or because he'd done all this so many times before? He had a good 20 years of leading man experience under his belt so probably had done hundreds of scenes like this. Pandora wondered how she measured up to the other famous actresses he'd been on top of.

Barclay had suggested the three of them go out to dinner to celebrate getting the scene in the bag, and Pandora gladly agreed. They could all do with letting off some steam.

She heard her phone ping and checked the screen. It was Clay asking her what time she'd be at the club tonight. Ugh, she'd forgotten about promising that. It was the last thing she felt like after the day she'd had. But she had promised him she'd show her face tonight.

Her fingers typed rapidly. *Sorry, working late. Not sure what time I'll get there.* It was a white lie, but after all, she was with colleagues, and they were bound to spend all evening discussing the movie, so it definitely counted as work. Besides, she could do with letting her hair down and relaxing. She spotted her wedding ring in front of the mirror and slipped it back onto her finger before fluffing her hair and going to meet the others.

Later Pandora sat in the cab, watching the bright lights of London slide by. They'd had a lovely dinner, the three of them talking about the scenes to come and laughing about all the issues that they'd had so far. It felt great to go out and be talking about something they were all so passionate about, something she couldn't do with Clay. Increasingly she felt she had less and less in common with him. He seemed to be making a point of not being interested in her career, as if he resented it, which she just didn't understand. *What had changed?*

But perhaps that was unfair. After all, she couldn't remember the last time she'd asked him about his work. Maybe they both needed to put a bit more effort in. She hadn't checked her phone while she was in the restaurant but now realised she'd had a couple more texts from him. She sighed. What she really wanted was a bath and an early night. It had been a long day.

She toyed with the idea of going home and getting dressed up, but she was too tired. She'd worn a jumper dress to work to avoid any marks on her body from jeans or underwear, and that should be smart enough. Clay would just have to take her as he found her.

Pandora stepped into the familiar surroundings of the club, forcing a smile on her face. Coming to the club felt like a chore, but as soon as she spotted Clay the familiar butterflies in her stomach fluttered, he turned and their eyes locked. He gave her a slow smile which she returned and all the resentment she'd been feeling evaporated. It was good to see him.

He crossed the room and caught her hand, leading her over to the private balcony. Once they were alone, he slid his arms around her and pulled her into an embrace. She felt the tensions of the day melt away as her body responded to him, the familiar heat returning.

"I can't wait for this bloody movie to be done, so we get to see each other again," he murmured.

Pandora frowned and pulled away. After all, she was working normal hours, although admittedly she'd stayed late today. Clay was the one that worked all evening and night. Why should she have to change what she was doing?

There was a bottle of champagne on ice, and she stepped back and opened it, pouring them both a drink. She bit her lip. She didn't want to get into another argument, not tonight.

"We haven't been out here since our wedding night," she smiled, remembering that perfect evening. "That awful journalist was asking you all those questions."

"And all I wanted to do was rip your clothes off."

The corner of her mouth twitched. "Me too. I always fancied having open-air sex but we hardly could with a news crew there."

"Well," said Clay moving over to the far side of the

balcony and beckoning, "there are no photographers here tonight, and if we move over here it's a lot more private. No one can see us unless they come and peer around the corner."

She grinned back at him, her heart racing. The possibility of being caught added an extra thrill, and she could tell he felt the same. She joined him, leaning back against the edge of the balcony, a shiver running through her as Clay slowly lowered the zip that ran down the front of her dress.

Clay's breath hitched as he discovered she was naked underneath. Pandora looked up at him, a smile tugging at her lips. He didn't need to know why she hadn't worn underwear, let him think she'd done it for him. She grasped his lapels and pulled him towards her. "Get here and warm me up. It's bloody freezing."

And in a second he closed the gap, his mouth on hers, cool hands running over the heat of her body. She quickly undid his tie and shirt and felt the warmth of his chest as it pressed against her. There was something more urgent pressing against her too, and she groaned in response. He was ready straight away, which suited her; she was ready too. After a bit of frantic fumbling with belts and buttons, Pandora wrapped her legs around Clay, and they cried out as they drew together. As they moved as one under the night sky, all resentments were forgotten, and everything felt right with the world again.

33
THAT'S A WRAP

Clay was feeling chipper. Life was about to get good, just the way he wanted it. Pandora's filming was coming to an end, and he'd have her all to himself again. The past few months had been tough; she'd been completely absorbed with this movie, barely coming into the club because she was tired and insisting she needed her beauty sleep. This wasn't what he'd signed up for.

If he was honest, he was feeling neglected and a bit disillusioned with married life. Pandora might be all his, but if he didn't see her, that wasn't much of a benefit. Plus, despite his efforts, she didn't seem to be pregnant yet, which was frustrating. He wondered whether there was something wrong with her. Women fell pregnant so easily, so why wasn't she? After all, he'd done everything he could to help the process along. He'd even spent a whole afternoon, when he was feeling particularly spiteful, going through their stash of condoms poking holes in the packets with a pin, and he thought that would have worked by now.

After all, she might not be planning on having a family

yet, but if she fell pregnant by accident, Clay was sure that would all change. Initially, it had annoyed him they needed to rely on condoms, but she'd said there was some medical reason for not being able to go on the pill and he'd had to accept that. But perhaps it hadn't been such a bad thing. His plan would have been much harder to put into action otherwise.

He'd hoped that by the time the movie finished shooting Pandora would be excitedly planning for the patter of tiny feet, but she still seemed to have her sights set on her movie career. Perhaps she just hadn't realised she was pregnant yet. He'd just have to be patient for a little longer.

The last day of filming was yesterday, and she was bringing some of her co-stars to the club to celebrate tonight. Clay had no interest in meeting them. He didn't care about movie stars or celebrities; he was just glad to be getting his wife back.

Annoyingly, however, Frankie was impressed by celebrities, so he was coming in tonight, looking forward to meeting some famous faces. And as he frequently said, it was all good publicity for the club. Clay rolled his eyes. *Did the man never think of anything else? The club was busy and making good money. Couldn't Frankie be happy with that?* There were more important things in life, after all.

Still, it was only for tonight, then he and Pandora could get back to normal.

Pandora was late, which was winding Clay up. He'd been in work since seven and was getting bored waiting for her to turn up. Admittedly she hadn't given him a specific time, but she'd said they would come around nine and it was already nearly half-past.

Plus Frankie was pacing anxiously and had already asked him what time the party were arriving. The reserved table in its prime location stuck out like a sore thumb. Every time Clay scanned the room; the empty table seemed to be mocking him. He poured himself a drink.

By the time Pandora eventually showed, looking glamorous and laughing with her friends, Clay was on his third drink and feeling pretty bloody resentful. She greeted him with a kiss, either oblivious to or ignoring his bad-mannered scowl, and introduced everyone to Barclay and Henri. Frankie was charm personified and ushered them over to their table, working his usual magic and shooting a warning glance back at Clay.

Clay downed his drink, his eyes narrowed, as he watched Frankie and Linda chatting to Pandora and her friends. *They certainly looked like they were getting on famously.* He hadn't realised Pandora had been hanging out with other men this whole time. Both Barclay and Henri were getting on a bit, but they were both attractive in a middle-aged way, and Pandora certainly seemed keen on them.

She turned and caught his eye, calling him over, and he sullenly went to join them. He supposed he'd better make an effort. After tonight they'd be shot of these tossers anyway.

Clay pulled up a chair between Pandora and Barclay, forcing the director to shuffle up sideways. As he did so, he saw Henri lean over and whisper something in Pandora's ear, making her giggle. Clay wasn't to know that Henri whispered how delicious her husband was and how lucky she was to be going home to him every night. He just saw them giggling, and it pissed him off.

Barclay, who was blessed with natural confidence and who never doubted his ability to control a situation, spotted Clay's irritation.

"I have to congratulate you," he said. "You're the luckiest man in the world having Pandora for a wife."

"I know," Clay replied, tight-lipped. He didn't need telling that his wife was attractive by another man. He didn't like it.

But Barclay thought complimenting Pandora was the way to win Clay over, so he kept going.

"I was taking a bit of a risk giving her a starring role, but she's proved she's got what it takes. I have to say she's been amazing. I'm starting work on another project soon, and I think she'd be perfect for it. Keep it between us, though; I haven't talked to her about it yet. I didn't want to distract her while we were filming."

Clay didn't respond so Barclay pushed on.

"It's an amazing role, with real Oscar potential, and I think she could surprise everyone. It could take her to the next level. I'm flying out to LA to start pre-production in a few weeks."

That got Clay's attention.

"LA?" he said, turning to face Barclay. "She's not fucking going to America."

Barclay made the mistake of laughing.

"Lighten up, man. You're the luckiest guy. Your wife is going to be the next big thing. You're going to have to learn to share her with the world. Your girl's going to be a star!"

Clay stood, his chair clattering to the floor. Barclay could see Clay was upset but had no idea why. He put a hand on Clay's shoulder.

"Come on, man. You should be pleased. You can always come with her."

Clay shrugged Barclay's hand away and hissed, "I won't be coming with her because she won't be fucking going."

Barclay looked uncomprehending. To him, nothing was more important than the work. Why didn't this man understand the opportunity he was giving Pandora? "What's the matter with you, man?"

Frankie, sensing trouble, rose to his feet, but before he could intervene, Clay's temper snapped, and he punched Barclay hard in the face sending him reeling backwards.

The whole room stilled as they watched to see what would happen next.

Pandora, her face a mask of horror, jumped up to go to Barclay, but Clay grabbed her wrist, pulling her towards the exit.

"Come on, we're going home," he said grimly.

She shook him off.

"No we're bloody well not," she said, going to a dazed and shocked Barclay who was sprawled on the floor. A cut under his eye was bleeding, and his face was starting to swell. He was looking at Clay in astonishment. This type of thing didn't happen to him.

Clay went to grab Pandora again, but Frankie placed himself between them. He didn't have to say anything; one look was enough to make Clay back down.

"Get out of here. Now."

Clay slunk away, angry and resentful. Glancing back over his shoulder, he could see everyone crowding around fucking Barclay.

That bitch, what did she think she was doing siding with him?

He was tempted to go back and give her a piece of his mind, but that would mean pitting himself directly against Frankie, and even in his drunken rage, he knew he'd regret that.

Clay returned to the office and, having poured himself a large Scotch, slumped in his chair, his thoughts seething.

If Clay was in a foul mood, it was nothing to the temper Frankie was in after seeing his special guests to a cab and apologising profusely for his employee's behaviour, as Clay could tell when Frankie stormed into the office and slammed the door behind him.

Clay woke the following morning in a foul temper, which only worsened once he realised Pandora wasn't there. *Hadn't she come home last night? Where the fuck was she?* He stalked around the flat looking for signs she'd come in late and just left early, but everything was untouched. There was no escaping the fact. She hadn't come home.

His anger rising, he tried calling her, but her phone went straight to voicemail. The bitch was punishing him for hitting her important director, he thought bitterly. She needed to rethink her priorities. Where the hell was she?

She was probably staying with Bea, but there was no way he was calling chasing after her. What would he say? *Do you know where my wife is?* There was no way he was doing that. He wasn't going to look like a fool.

She'd give in; she'd have to. After all, this was her home. And she'd miss him. She'd be back soon enough, and when she did, she'd have a lot of making up to do.

34
REGRET & RETALIATION

Pandora stretched luxuriously before realising that she wasn't in her own bed and sitting up with a start. *What the hell?* The sheets were satin, and the bed was huge. As she came to, the events of the previous night came flooding back, and she flopped back onto the bed and stared at the ceiling. Her mind roiled with conflicting emotions: anger at the way Clay had behaved, dread at his reaction to her going home with someone else, and embarrassment at having to face Barclay this morning, who she could hear moving around in the kitchen.

She'd have to face him, but at least there was an en-suite so she could freshen up first. She took a dressing gown from the back of the door and, after running a brush through her hair and washing her face, she padded cautiously out into the large open-plan living room.

Barclay turned, and Pandora winced before she could stop herself. His face was a mess - his eye was bloodshot, with a cut underneath surrounded by a swollen purple bruise. He smiled sheepishly and flinched as the movement sent pain shooting through his face. She rushed forward.

"I'm so sorry," she said mortified. "Is it very sore?"

"It's OK," he shrugged, "besides, you've got nothing to apologise for, it wasn't you that hit me."

"No, but..."

He waved away her protestations and handed her a coffee.

"Look. Forget what happened last night. It's not what's important. But you have some thinking to do. Whatever issues you and your husband have right now, you need to decide what you're going to do. He flew off the handle last night because I mentioned you doing a project in LA."

She frowned, "LA?"

He held his hands up apologetically. "I know, I know. I shouldn't have said something to him before I'd spoken to you. And I can fill you in on that later. My point is, that was his reaction to you moving to America, even for a few months. He doesn't seem like a guy who wants you to have a career. He wants you there with him, jealously guarded in his little world. And if you're happy with that, then that's fine by me, but I need to know. I can see a lot of potential in you, but I can't afford to invest in you and then have you drop out of a big movie because he's pressuring you to come home."

Pandora took a sip of coffee, feeling a familiar surge of anger at Clay's behaviour. He treated her like he owned her and she'd had enough of him trying to control her. She took a determined breath.

"If I have to choose between Clay and my career, there's no contest. Tell me about this project in LA."

Pandora and Barclay spent the day lounging around his penthouse flat, talking excitedly about his new movie as well as the post-production phase that he was about to start for *Lancelot*. Pandora found him a welcome relief from Clay, who had been so charming to begin with but who didn't share any of her interests, and who was making her feel increasingly claustrophobic. As her work schedule had increased, he had grown increasingly sullen, and she now realised she'd been avoiding talking about work just to keep him in a good mood.

The only thing they agreed on was sex, which was still as compulsive and heady as it ever had been. Perhaps that attraction was the only thing they ever really had in common. She couldn't imagine Clay ever moving out to LA with her, and she certainly wasn't planning to give up her career to become a good little housewife.

Had she just married him to spite her parents? He was certainly their worst nightmare. But then if she left him, she'd have a failed marriage behind her, and wouldn't that only prove them right?

No. She refused to let him clip her wings. She was being given a fantastic opportunity, and there was no way she was walking away from that. Besides she'd be miserable if she stayed here and gave up her dreams, and that would sour everything between them anyway. If she was honest with herself, things already had soured.

It would never work, and now he'd shown his true colours. It was better that she just cut her losses now.

Perhaps it was inevitable that Pandora and Barclay would end up in bed. They'd always got on, and she'd found him attractive in a sophisticated, older-man kind of way, but they'd both been too busy working ever to consider taking it further. Besides, there had been Clay to think about.

But as they lounged around laughing and discussing films, both of them dressed only in dressing gowns, Pandora started to see him differently. He was so vital and passionate about the same things she was. Plus, he was incredibly supportive and understood her professional ambitions, something Clay had never done. She'd found a kindred spirit.

So maybe it wasn't surprising that things would progress, although when they did, it took both of them by surprise. Pandora had an excellent idea for a *Lancelot* promo and grabbed Barclay's knee excitedly, making his dressing gown slip to one side, and they both felt the atmosphere shift. After a few tense seconds, she leaned in and kissed him. It was a leap into the unknown. But it was also a way of closing one door and opening another.

Barclay, who believed an artistic spirit should be free and easy, had responded enthusiastically, before pulling back and asking Pandora if she was sure she wanted to do this. She answered by shrugging her gown to the floor and leading him towards the bedroom.

Afterwards, they dozed peacefully entwined in the rumpled satin sheets, and when Pandora awoke, she felt lighter, as if she'd shed some emotional baggage. There wasn't the same intense attraction she felt with Clay, but Barclay was a considerate lover and, all things considered, she felt great. A tension she hadn't even noticed before had lifted.

She hadn't just slept with Barclay; she'd made a decision. There was no going back now, and that felt good.

The question foremost in her mind was how to resolve things with Clay as quickly and painlessly as possible. She left Barclay sleeping and quietly slipped on the dressing gown. Padding into the living room she sat on the sofa, curled her legs underneath her and, bracing herself, turned on her phone. *Fifteen messages.*

She listened to them, her face grim. With every message Clay left, he became drunker and more abusive, before phasing through apologising and sobbing, then turning angry once again. Pandora listened to every word then deleted the messages and sat staring blankly in front of her.

She had to tell him it was over, but his messages just confirmed it wouldn't be easy and she dreaded the scene he would cause. She didn't know whether he'd be defensive, angry, upset, pleading, and she couldn't face any of those right now. Perhaps a few days apart would give him time to calm down and get used to her not being around.

She switched her phone off and went back into the bedroom, smiling as she saw Barclay was stirring. She slid the dressing gown to the floor and slipped back into bed.

35
OPPORTUNITIES & INCONVENIENCES

Despite its disastrous start, Pandora and Barclay had a great weekend. Barclay revealed more about his new project, and Pandora got increasingly excited about it. They were stuck in the flat unless Pandora wanted to wear the dress she'd worn at the party, but that suited them just fine. They moved from the sofa to the bed to eating takeaways in front of the enormous TV.

Pandora tried not to think about Monday morning and what lay ahead of her; after all, she couldn't live in Barclay's dressing gown forever. She needed to end it with Clay and move her stuff out of the flat, but the thought of seeing him filled her with dread, and also she had nowhere to go. So she was delighted when Barclay's assistant, Ashton, turned up on Sunday evening with shopping bags filled with enough new clothes to last her a fortnight.

She protested, shocked at Barclay's generosity, and said she couldn't possibly accept anything, but Ashton had simply raised an eyebrow and given her a sharp look up and down. "Really? I'm guessing you won't be going out like that baby girl. It looks to me like it's a good job I've come to the rescue. Besides, it's all on tick against the film budget so keep whatever you like and the rest I'll just send back."

She gave him a grateful hug and rushed off to look through the bags of shopping. It felt like Christmas morning, and Ashton had fabulous taste. She loved pretty much everything.

After the last few months on set, he'd obviously got a good sense for what she liked, and suddenly she felt liberated. The thought that she could avoid going back to the flat for a few more days lifted a weight from her shoulders. She could leave it a bit longer before she had to face Clay.

Sadly, no matter how life-altering Pandora's weekend had been Monday morning came round fast. Barclay's rare break from work was over, and he was starting a gruelling post-production schedule. Much to Pandora's delight, he invited her to go along and see the process, but she had to decline. She would have loved to and assured him she would go with him another day, but she had some urgent things to get done today.

As soon as he left, she tugged on a pair of jeans, pulled a baseball cap on over her hair and nipped out to the chemist around the corner. Within 15 minutes, she was back in the flat and staring at the positive pregnancy test in her hands.

How the hell had this happened? They had always been so careful about protection. She felt a flash of annoyance as she remembered Clay's belly-aching about having to use a condom, but she had always insisted. She shook the thought out of her head. She was done being annoyed with Clay. That part of her life was over.

Pandora switched her phone on, bracing herself for the onslaught of abusive voicemails, but to her surprise, there had been no calls.

All the same, she didn't want to leave her phone on right now. She couldn't face an unexpected call from Clay, not with what she had ahead of her this afternoon. She'd turn it back off as soon as she'd looked something up. She opened a browser and started searching for a local clinic with a walk-in service.

When Barclay returned late that evening, he found Pandora fast asleep in bed. Suffering terrible stomach cramps, she'd taken some painkillers and was sleeping them off. She'd sent him a text earlier saying she wasn't feeling well and, after checking on her, he took a blanket and went and slept on the sofa. He didn't want to wake her if she was sick, and he couldn't afford to catch anything. He had too much work to do.

She woke the following morning to find herself alone again but with freshly brewed coffee in the pot and a bag of croissants on the counter. She bit into one and groaned with pleasure, she'd barely eaten the previous day and was starving.

Grateful to have the flat to herself - she didn't want to explain why she'd been feeling unwell - she pulled on some jeans and wandered into Barclay's study. He'd left a note saying the script for the new movie was in there if she wanted to take a look, so she poured herself a coffee, made a hot water bottle to ease her aching stomach and went to have a read.

It was hours before she emerged. By the time she did she'd read the whole script from start to finish without pausing. It was gripping. Harrowing and raw and challenging, but it would make a fantastic movie. Did he really think she could pull off a part like this?

It was a total departure from anything she'd done before. There was no glamour and no sexy costumes or beautiful makeup.

She could see why he'd called it Oscar bait. It would be

a tough movie to film, but if she could pull it off, it would launch her as a serious actress. It was a hell of an opportunity, and only confirmed she'd made the right decision yesterday, no matter how difficult it had been.

36
GOING LOCO

Nearly a week after that night at the club Clay was still wondering where the hell his wife was. Angry and embittered, he was drinking too much, and his temper was on a hair-trigger. Everyone was keeping out of his way. When he did turn up to work, he was late and then did precious little. He just sat at the bar, drinking it dry.

He woke late, his mouth dry and his head fuzzy, as he had done every morning since Pandora had left. He needed a fry-up. That would make him feel better. He was still wearing the clothes from the night before, but he didn't care. *What did it matter anyway?*

Pulling the door closed behind him, he stumbled down the street as far as the greasy spoon and ordered himself breakfast. He sat drinking a cup of tea and flicked absent-mindedly through a newspaper. There was nothing that piqued his interest - politics, a busty TV presenter photographed in a bikini on holiday and a scandal about a businessman who'd broken a bank. He couldn't care less. Then on page five, he spotted a familiar face.

He jolted upright, sloshing tea all over the paper, and

took a closer look. *That bitch.*

Pandora's new love nest! Months after marrying her East End gangster boyfriend, rising star Pandora Caine is rumoured to be shacked up with Hollywood Director Barclay Soames. The pair have been pictured out and about, and she's been spotted leaving his apartment early in the morning.

Clay growled, drawing alarmed glances from the other people in the café.

What the hell was she thinking? How dare she go off with somebody else?

He quickly scanned the rest of the article and discovered that Barclay's flat was in Mayfair (of course it bloody was) and squinted closely at a blurred photo of Pandora wearing a baseball cap stepping through the doorway. It wasn't the best picture, but it was definitely her. He stood, his chair making a loud screech, and stormed out of the café.

That bitch was going to get a piece of his mind.

It didn't take Clay more than an hour to find Barclay's flat. Mayfair wasn't a large place, and he recognised the building from the photo.

Not pausing to think, he stormed inside but faltered as he found himself in the lobby. There were half a dozen flats in the building, and he had no idea which was Barclay's. A bored security guard glanced up at him, his eyes narrowing suspiciously as he took in the wild-eyed man standing before him.

"Can I help you, sir?"

Clay wasn't sure what to do. The guard was on the wrong side of middle age and carrying some extra weight, so he wasn't a threat, but there was no way Clay was getting up to see Pandora without being buzzed in. He needed to be clever about this. He didn't want the guy phoning up and warning her that he was here. She'd refuse to see him, or call the police, he thought bitterly.

"Nah mate," he said, with a flash of the old charm.

"I've got the wrong place, sorry." And with a shake of his head, he laughed and walked back out onto the street.

He'd wait until she came out. There was a pub across the street. He'd sit in there and watch the entrance. Besides, he was thirsty.

The daylight faded to darkness, and Clay was the best part through a bottle of whiskey before he saw anything of interest.

Sitting at a table by the window, he had a good view of the building opposite, but could also see a billboard emblazoned with Pandora's fragrance ad. In the photo, she gazed directly at him, lips parted, as she caressed a bottle of perfume, her huge face seeming to mock him from on high. And that just made him angrier.

It was around seven when he saw a man get out of a cab and walk into the building. *Had that been the fucking yank?* Clay couldn't be sure, but he thought it was.

He watched the windows to see which flat the guy went into, but no new lights went on, so it was impossible to tell.

His mind buzzed with frustration as the minutes stretched, and his traitorous mind imagined what was going on in the flat above - Pandora welcoming Barclay home, just like she used to with him. That guy's hands all over her body, his lips on hers. The glass in his hand shattered, and he swore. A red line of blood grew where the glass had cut him. He balled his fist. *He'd kill them.* But he needed them to come out first.

Clay's temper wasn't improved since he was now unable to leave his table to get another drink in case he missed them. So he sat, leg jiggling impatiently, his eyes never leaving the entrance.

It wasn't long before his patience was rewarded. In a little under half an hour, he spotted movement in the lobby and jumped to his feet.

They were coming out.

Pandora and Barclay were oblivious to the impending danger as they stepped onto the pavement, smiling and holding hands. Barclay had left work at a reasonable time for once and booked them a table at a local restaurant. They would walk, it wasn't far, and it was a lovely evening.

They both froze as Clay stepped into their path.

Pandora slipped her hand out of Barclay's and stared in dismay at the man before her. He was barely recognisable as the man she'd fallen in love with. He was unshaven, drunk and looked like he hadn't showered for days. His eyes were bloodshot, and his face, which she'd thought so handsome, was now distorted by hate.

Her first reaction was to back away and bolt back inside, but then a surge of resentment washed over her, and she stood her ground. He'd nearly ruined everything for her, and she refused to let him drag her down any more. The last thing she wanted was a confrontation in the street, but things needed saying, and she could say them here as well as anywhere.

"You bitch," he hissed.

She looked unimpressed. Her voice level, she said, "What are you doing here, Clay?"

"I can't believe you shacked up with this fucking idiot. I should have known you'd sleep with anyone to get ahead; it's what everyone says about you."

Her eyes narrowed. That was a low blow. He knew how upset she'd been after the incident with Crowder in that hotel room, and even though she knew his comments were calculated to hurt her, they still stung. Much to her irritation, she felt tears welling in her eyes, but that only hardened her resolve. She would not let him get the better of her. He was just a small-minded bully.

"You know that's not true. How can you say that after what happened?"

He laughed. "Yeah, and who sorted that out for you?"

She frowned, uncomprehending, and his face twisted

into a nasty grin. "Oh, you thought it was a coincidence that he ended up with a knife in his ribs, did you?"

Pandora paled, horrified, and took a step backwards. Her eyes searched Clay's as she tried to work out whether he was telling the truth. She saw nothing but defiance and pride. Her heart sank. *What the hell had he done?* Yes, Crowder was a creep and a sex-pest, but she'd never imagined Clay had killed him.

Clay chuckled nastily and shook his head.

"You just don't know what's good for you do you? Why couldn't you just get pregnant and settle down like a normal woman? There must be something wrong with you if you're not expecting by now."

Fear turned to fury as Pandora realised that he'd been trying to trick her into getting pregnant all along. *How could he?* They'd talked about it, and she'd said she wasn't ready to have a family. She'd assumed that he would respect that, but clearly he hadn't.

She thought about the clinic, the numb sadness she'd felt as she aborted the pregnancy he'd forced upon her and she felt a white-hot anger rush through her. But she knew telling Clay she'd had a termination would push him too far. She had to resist the urge to throw that in his face, no matter how much she felt like hurting him right now. Instead, she stood strong and forced a calm she didn't feel into her voice.

"It's over Clay. I want a divorce."

He lurched forward and grabbed her by the chin, forcing her head up. She stared back at him defiantly.

"It's over when I say it's over."

At this point, Barclay intervened to get Clay to let go of her, which worked for Clay as he suddenly had a new target. And now he didn't need to hold back. Clay smirked as he saw the now greenish bruise on Barclay's face.

"Come back for more have you?" he grinned, before headbutting the unsuspecting Barclay. Barclay reeled backwards clutching his nose. It would have been far worse if Clay hadn't been drunk, but it still bloody hurt. Pandora dropped to Barclay's side, trying to stem the blood streaming from his broken nose.

Clay roughly shoved her out of the way and pulled Barclay to his feet. It was then that the security guard stepped in. As Clay had previously assessed, the guy was out of shape, but still big enough to give Clay momentary pause. It was in the brief silence that they heard police sirens approaching.

Clay didn't care; he wanted revenge.

37
STEPPING UP

Frankie sat on the sofa, his arm around Linda, as he enjoyed a brief moment of peace. The kids were in bed; even the baby had started sleeping through the night. Linda snuggled against him and sighed contentedly. He kissed her hair and smiled to himself. Moments like this made it all worthwhile.

So it was with great annoyance that he answered his phone a few seconds later. Linda looked up at him, silently pleading for him not to go anywhere.

"Yes, Stanley?"

'Sorry to bother you, Mr Finch, but I thought you should know. Clay didn't come into work yesterday, and he hasn't shown up tonight either."

Frankie didn't say anything. Clay not showing wasn't a huge surprise, Frankie knew he had gone a bit off the rails recently.

"You did ask me to keep you informed," said Stanley apologetically, "and it's due to be a busy night tonight."

Frankie heaved a sigh and pinched the bridge of his nose. Clay was proving to be a real fucking liability.

"Thanks for letting me know," he said and shut off the call.

He started to get up with great reluctance.

"Can't you send Chris to sort it out?" complained Linda. "Besides, if you stay here I could make it worth your while?" she said, wiggling her eyebrows.

Frankie considered. He looked down at his wife, who had been exhausted since the baby was born, and liked the spark of excitement he saw in her eyes. Besides, heading down to the club right now was the last thing he wanted to do. Perhaps he could send Chris. The boy had proved himself. Maybe it was time to give the lad a bit more responsibility.

Clay woke in a police cell. The custody officer who came to check on him was gratingly cheery, offering him a cup of tea, and asking him how his head felt this morning with a hearty chuckle. Clay sighed and accepted a cuppa. He knew better than to rant and rail against the police; he'd only be in here longer. Once they were satisfied that he'd sobered up, he was released with a caution. It seemed that Barclay hadn't wanted to press charges. That probably meant he hadn't hurt him enough, which was disappointing.

Clay had a long walk home, and he set off, head down, wanting nothing more than his own bed or another drink. As he trudged the quiet streets, the events of the previous evening reasserted themselves, and he decided blotting out those memories was more important than sleeping. He felt dreadful. Hungover, with a side order of sadness and regret, plus a lurking fear about the repercussions of telling Pandora he'd killed Crowder. Had he really said that? He should have kept his fucking mouth shut. She'd always have that over him now.

At least she hadn't said anything to the police yet; otherwise, he'd be in an interview room instead of walking home. He supposed he'd got off lightly. But it didn't feel like that.

He found himself wishing for Ivy. Sweet, undemanding Ivy who would always listen to him. He should never have fired her. That was Pandora's fault. She'd ruined the one true friendship he'd ever had. Now she'd left him, and he couldn't even go and talk to Ivy about it. Not after everything that had happened. Ivy wouldn't let him in the door.

So with nowhere else to go, he headed to the nearest pub, which was just opening. A landlord was always guaranteed to make you feel welcome. It was either that or head back to his empty flat, which was full of reminders of Pandora.

But instead of making him feel better, the pint of beer seemed to bring it all back into focus, his anger and humiliation returning. He downed the pint and decided to keep on walking, his mind churning, reliving the events of the night before. His brain was still seething as he let himself into his flat and threw his coat down on the floor. *How could Pandora say it was over?*

He spotted a pair of her shoes in the corner of the room, abandoned there weeks before. The memory of her dancing barefoot towards him, swaying her hips and beckoning swam before his eyes. He shook his head and stomped into the kitchen, pulling a bin liner from under the sink. He shoved the shoes inside, then added the jacket she'd left hanging in the hall. He moved into the bedroom, and emptied the racks of clothes from the wardrobe, stuffing them unceremoniously into bin bags. *She always had too many fucking clothes. Well, she wouldn't be getting these back.* He heaved the bags downstairs and dumped them on the street.

Reentering, he stood catching his breath, surveying the flat. It looked stark and empty, but it was free of her. And that felt good. She was out of his life. She could go and rot for all he cared. He poured himself a large glass of whiskey. It was time to celebrate.

A short while later Clay peered at himself in the bathroom mirror, his reflection swimming in front of him. He had a shower, narrowly avoiding slipping as he got out, and giggled to himself. *Oops, that could have been a disaster!* He could have ended up looking as banged-up as Barclay if he hadn't caught himself! He pulled on a fresh suit and knocked back another Scotch.

He was going to his club. Back where he belonged. He'd wasted enough time and energy on Pandora, and he was ready to get back out there and play the field. He smiled as he thought of the many happy conquests he'd had there, and wondered what beautiful girl would take his eye tonight.

It was Chris's second night overseeing the club. He'd been quite shocked when Frankie had asked him to take the reins yesterday, although he'd tried to look like he was taking it in his stride. It was a big responsibility. But he would do Frankie proud; it was the least he could do.

Stanley had been surprised to see Chris. After calling Frankie he'd been expecting the big man himself to show up, or even to be put in charge himself, but he just shrugged and accepted the new status quo. There was no way he was arguing with a man-mountain like Chris. Besides, if that was what Frankie wanted, it was OK with him.

There wasn't a great deal for Chris to do other than keeping an eye on proceedings and making sure there were no issues. He didn't drink, he didn't socialise, but he kept things running smoothly, and it was with a sense of relief and satisfaction that he locked up after everyone had gone. Little did he know, his second night would be a very different experience.

Everything was going well until Clay walked in. Chris spotted him immediately and could see he was hammered. He squared his shoulders and walked over.

Clay was leaning on the bar, drink already in hand

when he felt Chris looming over him. He looked Chris up and down in slow disbelief.

"What the fuck are you doing here?" he slurred.

"Frankie sent me to keep an eye on things."

"What the fuck's he done that for? Well, you can fuck off. I'm here now."

"I don't think so. You're drunk, and I think you should go home," he said, putting a hand on Clay's shoulder to steer him towards the door.

"Get your fucking hands off me!" Clay reacted, shrugging him off and swinging a wild punch.

Chris avoided it with minimal effort; Clay was far too intoxicated to manage any effective attack. It was with a slight sigh of resignation that he hit Clay with a sharp uppercut, taking him down like a tonne of bricks.

There were a few startled *Oh!s* behind him and Chris turned around, his hands raised in a placatory gesture. "Nothing to see here folks, he's just had one too many. Carry on with your evening."

With the help of Stanley, who was now feeling incredibly grateful that Chris was in charge instead of him, they dragged the unconscious Clay out of sight and dialled Frankie.

To say Frankie was unimpressed was the understatement of the century. His face was thunderous when he arrived. He wasn't angry with Chris. In fact, Chris had done a blinding job and avoided what could have been a major incident. It was Clay that Frankie was annoyed with.

Leaving Stanley in charge, the two of them bundled Clay into the car and drove him home, heaving him upstairs and dumping him unceremoniously on the bed. They both stood looking down at him. "Fucking idiot," said Frankie, shaking his head.

"Do you think we should leave him on his own?" said Chris staring at the unresponsive figure sprawled on the duvet. "We don't want him choking on his own vomit."

"Or getting back up and carrying on drinking," said Frankie dryly. Personally, he wouldn't be too fussed if Clay choked, at least he'd stop being a pain in the arse, but he supposed Chris had a point. He pulled out his phone and flicked through his contacts. The call took a while to be answered, and Frankie paced impatiently as he waited, but then it was a bit late for polite phone calls.

"Mrs Caulder?" Frankie said. Chris could hear a squawking from the other end of the phone. "No, not to worry, Clay's fine, but he's got himself into a bit of a state. His drinking's got a bit out of hand, and I'd like you to come and keep an eye on him."

Frankie listened and nodded. "Yes, we're at his flat. We'll wait till you get here, but make it sharpish, will you?" His phone beeped, and he glanced at the screen. "I've got another call coming in. See you shortly."

Frankie ended the call and answered the waiting one.

"Yes, Stanley?"

Stanley's panicked voice sounded frantic. "Mr Finch, you need to get down here right away. It's awful. Its Big Arf, he's been stabbed."

Frankie's face set in a grim line. He strode back into the bedroom and looked down at the gently snoring Clay. *Pathetic.*

Frankie slapped him round the face, and Clay came to, squinting in the bright bedroom light, his expression turning from confusion to horror as he recognised Frankie looking down at him.

He immediately went on the defensive.

"What the hell? That wanker Chris hit me, in my own club! Fucking hell Frankie, what the fuck?"

Frankie held a finger to his lips, and Clay shut up.

"Listen to me, Clay. I know you've had a rough few weeks, but this is an end to it, you understand? You're a fucking liability. I don't want to see you again until you're sober and you've sorted your head out. I don't care what's happened. It ends now. Understood?"

Clay nodded meekly.

"And another thing. It's my club, not yours, you little prick. And from now on it's under new management. You're not fit to wipe your own arse at the moment, let alone run a club. Let me be clear. If I hear you've caused even the smallest bit of trouble, or gone within a hundred yards of that club, I'll come looking for you. Have you got that?"

Frankie walked out. Clay groaned and curled into a ball. He could hear talking in the next room and a woman's voice, then receding footsteps and the front door closing. *Oh, Christ was that his mum?* He covered his face with a pillow. He couldn't believe Frankie had called his mum to come and look after him, could this get any more humiliating? As if taunting him, his stomach answered that question, and he ran stumbling and retching towards the bathroom.

38
COUNTERATTACK

Frankie had had enough. He'd spent the night at the hospital with Big Arf whose life was hanging in the balance. After five hours in surgery, Arf was now enjoying a heavily medicated sleep. He was expected to pull through, but it had been a close-run thing. Frankie leaned against the coffee machine, waiting while liquid dribbled into a flimsy plastic cup. His mind was whirling. Witnesses said the guy had shouted something that sounded like Albanian before running off, but why the hell would the Albanians attack his club? They must know he would retaliate. Did they want an all-out war?

Frankie roared and thumped the machine drawing startled glances. He took the steaming cup from the machine, raising it to his lips, then paused with it an inch away from his mouth, his face scrunching in disgust. *What the fuck was that smell?*

He peered at the contents of the cup and saw an unappetising pale liquid with bits in it. The fucking machine had dispensed instant chicken soup instead of coffee. He took a deep breath through his nose, turning his head to one side to avoid the foul-smelling liquid. *Fucking hell you'd have to be really desperate to drink that.* He rifled through his pockets, but that had been the last of his change, so he returned to the ward and handed the cup to Big Arf's wife. She gave him a grateful smile and took a sip. "Thanks, Mr Finch, that's just the ticket."

"Let me know if there's anything you need, OK, Pam?"

She nodded and grasped his hand. "Thanks," she said, tears welling in her eyes.

Oh for fuck's sake. The last thing he needed was a blubbing woman right now. He gave her a brusque nod and stalked out. Never had there been a man worse equipped to deal with female emotions. He needed to get out there and do something. Or hurt someone. The Albanians wouldn't get away with this.

Dawn was breaking, leaving a pink smudge across the London sky as Frankie returned to his car. He peered through the window to see Chris fast asleep with his mouth open in the driver's seat. He snorted and rapped on the glass. Chris blearily opened an eye then jumped to attention and quickly unlocked the doors.

"Wakey wakey Chris, we've got places to be."

"Sorry, Mr Finch," said Chris stifling a yawn. "How's Big Arf?"

"He'll pull through, but that still leaves us with a major problem. I don't know what the Albanians are thinking of attacking us unprovoked, but it can't go unpunished."

"What's the plan?"

"I have no fucking idea." Frankie massaged his forehead, trying to shift his headache. "My first thought was to hit them back, take a couple of their key men down. It'll escalate but perhaps at this stage that's inevitable. Maybe they haven't realised how badly that would end for them. But they poked the bear. We need to retaliate."

"Won't that cause as many problems for us as for them?"

Frankie pinched the bridge of his nose. He was too tired to be thinking straight right now. Chris had a point; an all-out gang-war was a hassle he didn't need. The police were turning a blind eye to Frankie's business dealings right now, but that would only continue if it were to their benefit.

Since Frankie had taken over from the Dixons a few years back, crime was down in the area. People were far more frightened of pissing Frankie off than they ever had been of being caught by the police. And because of that, the crime figures were down, which made the police's job easier. It suited both of them. But if dead gangsters started cropping up, that would change dramatically.

"Let's go home. I need breakfast and a decent cup of coffee. Then we work out what our next move is, and fast. Plus I don't want Linda and the kids on their own right now, just in case the Albanians really have lost their minds and decide to do something suicidal. A shadow passed over his face as old memories resurfaced. "In fact, put your foot down, will you? Let's get back home pronto."

39
RUIN & ROCK BOTTOM

Clay opened his eyes a fraction against the sunlight streaming through his bedroom window and saw that his mum had just set a cup of milky sweet tea by the side of the bed. He let out a moan as the events of the previous night came flooding back, then caught a whiff of the tea, and his stomach turned over. He pulled the duvet back over his head and closed his eyes.

But his stomach wasn't done with him, and instead of going back to sleep, he found himself stumbling desperately towards the bathroom and retching until his stomach was empty. He gripped the toilet bowl, panting and sweating, feeling about as miserable as it was possible to feel.

He'd lost everything. Pandora, the club, and any respect he'd had amongst the people who worked there. And after mouthing off about murdering Crowder, he might end up in prison too.

After a few minutes, he stood, shaky and shivering. He looked at his face in the mirror: the scar standing out red against his grey skin. He looked like shit.

He remembered the look on Pandora's face when he told her what he'd done. Stupidly he'd thought she would be pleased, flattered even that he'd done that for her, but she'd been horrified, frightened of him. There was no coming back from that, even if he wanted to. He'd ruined everything.

40
LET'S DANCE

It was gone midday when Frankie and Chris strode into the massage parlour. The hard-faced madam was behind the counter, and there was an unshaven man in a dark suit slouched in a chair. Both looked lazily up, and Frankie could practically see the adrenaline shoot into their bloodstreams once they clocked who'd walked in. The man clumsily reached for a bulge inside his jacket. But Chris spotted the movement and put him out like a light. He slumped and clattered to the floor. Chris disarmed him and stood with his back against the door. The madam stood her ground, her eyes like flint.

"What you want?" she said.

Frankie leaned into her, his voice low. "I want you to pass on a message. I don't know what the fuck you're thinking of attacking my club, but you've got one chance to fix it. If it was some rogue kid being a hero you've got until the end of the day to deal with him and make amends. Otherwise, I'm coming for you. And I mean all of you. You've got it good at the moment, but don't for one second think I won't put down every fucking Albanian in the area if this isn't fixed."

She sneered. "You thought there would be no payback for you killing that kid? The police might think he ran, but we know what happened."

Frankie slammed both his hands down on the counter, his face inches away from hers. She pulled back a fraction, but her expression remained implacable. "That little shit killed his mother," he said, jabbing his finger towards Chris. "If you thought there wouldn't be consequences, you don't know who you're fucking dealing with."

Her eyes widened slightly, betraying a flicker of fear for the first time.

Frankie pulled back. "You pass this on. And that means I'm making you responsible. You've got till the end of today, or you're not going to know what fucking hit you."

41
HOLLYWOOD REBOOT

Pandora's mouth gaped as the chauffeur eased the stately Maybach through the gates to Barclay's LA mansion. It took a while to cruise up the driveway through beautifully manicured tropical gardens before arriving at an expansive white-pillared house. It looked rather like a wedding cake, which reminded her briefly of Clay and how happy they'd been on their wedding day. She felt a pang of sadness but shook it off. She was rid of him, and she wouldn't let him spoil this for her.

Barclay glanced across and smiled at her wide-eyed wonder. "What do you think?"

"Amazing! I wasn't expecting this," she breathed.

He jumped out of the car, as excited as a five-year-old on Christmas morning. "Come on, let me show you around."

As they toured the house, she rapidly ran out of superlatives as they went from one luxurious room to another. There was a pool in the garden, a gym, home cinema and more bedrooms than she could count. She playfully tried to pull him into one of them, but he laughed and resisted.

"I hate to do this to you Dora honey, but I need to work today. I've got a crazy work schedule to get post-production done so I can get the wheels moving on the next movie."

She pouted. She wasn't used to being turned down. He squeezed her cheeks and chuckled. "That won't work with me, I'm afraid. The work has always been my first love. Get yourself unpacked and go and explore. Take a dip in the pool, relax, unwind. I'll leave the car for you. My man will take you anywhere you want to go."

With that, he winked at her and strode off, shouting back over his shoulder. "I'll be working until late. Why don't you give Henri a call? He lives nearby. See if he can introduce you to some people?"

Pandora walked to the window and watched as Barclay backed a bright red Porsche out of the garage and swept out of the driveway scattering gravel in his wake. She suddenly felt very alone. *That wouldn't do.* Pulling out her phone, she dialled Henri.

"Hi, Darling!" she purred. "I don't suppose you're around today? I've just arrived in LA and have nothing to do!"

Her face brightened. "You will? Brilliant! Yes, I'm at Barclay's. See you in a bit."

She grinned. Thank goodness for Henri. She'd better jump in the shower and smarten herself up before he picked her up. *Now, what should Hollywood's latest star wear to explore her new domain? Something sensational, of course! This town wasn't going to know what had hit it.*

42
ALBANIAN GIRL

Frankie's house was busier than usual. He'd put everyone on alert on his return from the massage parlour, apart from Linda, to whom he was still insisting there was nothing wrong.

As well as upping the protection at the club and the rest of his businesses, he'd called in the Winchester brothers who were currently lounging around in his kitchen. Big, broad and identical twins they were good muscle to have around. Plus they finished each other's sentences which was kind of sweet. Frankie wasn't taking any chances. Not this time, not when it came to his family.

Linda wasn't happy. It was clear something was going on, and she was getting increasingly pissed off that Frankie was treating her like some backward child, but she didn't want to cause a scene, not with so many people in the house.

It was 8pm when the doorbell rang. Everyone tensed. They'd ordered pizza ten minutes ago, but it was too early for that to arrive, and they weren't expecting anyone else. They were all feeling jumpy. Frankie jerked his head in the direction of the door, and the Winchester boys got up to answer it. Everyone in the kitchen fell silent and listened. Frankie could hear raised voices and strained to hear what was going on.

"You'd better come and see this, Frankie."

He turned to Linda and Chris. "You two stay here, understand?"

Linda looked peeved, and Chris gave him a curt nod.

Frankie wasn't sure what he was expecting, but it certainly wasn't what he found. There were two Albanians on the doorstep arguing with his guys, who looked baffled. Between them stood a skinny, blank-faced girl wearing a boob tube and a stretchy lurex mini skirt. She was shivering and couldn't be much older than 18. Everyone fell silent as Frankie approached.

"What the fuck is this?" said Frankie, lowering his voice to a hoarse whisper. The last thing he wanted was Linda barging out of the kitchen and seeing this.

"Go on," prompted one of the Winchesters.

The Albanian looked at Frankie, his face expressionless. "Our boss. He would like to apologise for the misunderstanding. He says the killing of the sick woman; it was unsanctioned. He did not know about it. He thought you killed his guy for no reason. So he made his point. He was misinformed. So he sends you this gift." The man gestured to the girl. "He doesn't want war."

Frankie stared incredulously at the girl then back to the man.

"What the fuck am I supposed to do with her?"

The Albanian shrugged. "Do what you like."

Frankie looked the girl up and down as she stared vacantly ahead. She was no honey trap; he wasn't even sure she knew what was happening. She'd probably come over to Britain in the hope of a new life, a bright new future but had long since lost any hope of that. He studied her face. There was no attitude, no pretence. She wasn't interested in flirting with him or pleasing him. He guessed experience had shown her that men would take what they wanted with or without any encouragement from her.

The men she'd been with, and he was guessing there had been a steady stream of them since she'd arrived, hadn't needed more than her basic compliance. And some probably hadn't even wanted that.

The silence stretched.

"In our country, it's an insult to turn down a gift. Our boss, he says you like our girls. You paid 20 grand for one a few weeks ago." He smirked, and Frankie started forward, sorely tempted to wipe that expression off his face, but he caught a reaction from the girl, the fear that she'd be rejected and what she would face if that happened. He saw the bruise marks in the shape of fingers on her arms and hesitated, then felt a movement behind him.

"Let her in," said Linda.

The Albanian's eyes widened in amused surprise, and Frankie threw Linda a look, frustrated that she hadn't stayed in the kitchen.

The girl stepped over the threshold, and Frankie slammed the door.

He turned to Linda. "What the hell? I thought you were staying in the kitchen?"

Linda gave him a look then turned to the twins. "Take her into the living room and keep an eye on her. Frankie, I want a word with you."

Frankie trailed behind her, feeling like he was on his way to the headmaster's office. Life looked like it was about to become a whole lot more complicated, which wasn't what he needed right now.

Linda opened the fridge, getting out ham, cheese and butter and started making sandwiches. She had a houseful of people, and in a crisis, people needed feeding.

Frankie watched her in silence until she'd stacked two large plates with sandwiches.

"Chris, take this into the other room and make sure that girl eats something. She looks like she hasn't had a decent meal in months."

Once Chris had left, she turned to Frankie, arms crossed.

"I think you'd better tell me what the hell has been going on Frankie Finch. And don't even think about leaving out the part where you paid twenty grand for some girl."

Frankie leaned against the work surface, studying his shoes. There was no getting around this. The truth wasn't good, but it was nowhere near as bad as she was imagining. He had no choice but to tell her the whole story.

By the time he finished, she had a deep frown on her face and had eaten three sandwiches without even noticing.

"Do you think that's it then? Was that a genuine attempt to call a truce?"

Frankie shrugged. "I think so. I'm as surprised as you. I certainly didn't expect that," he said, gesturing towards the living room.

Chris chose that moment to amble in and grab some drinks out of the fridge.

"What's going on in there?"

"Not much. She's sitting there looking scared, and the boys are watching her like you said."

Linda rolled her eyes. *Honestly, if you want something doing properly.* "What do they think she's going to do? It's not like she's got any concealed weapons in that outfit is it?"

Shaking her head in frustration at the general uselessness of the men in her life, she strode out of the room, her heels clacking on the tiled floor.

Frankie and Chris exchanged a look, and Frankie gave a small shrug. He knew better than to try and stop her. This was why he didn't want her to get involved.

Linda swung open the living room door startling everyone

inside. She nodded to the twins.

"Go on, piss off you two."

They hesitated. After all, Frankie had told them to keep an eye on the girl, but Linda raised an eyebrow, tapping her foot, and they decided they'd rather take their chances.

Once they had gone, she held out a sweatshirt and some leggings. The girl hesitated, looking confused, and Linda smiled sadly. "Put those on love; you must be freezing."

Linda perched on the arm of the sofa and watched as the girl hurriedly pulled the clothes on. Linda tried not to wince at the bruises that were revealed as she got changed.

The girl sat with her arms wrapped around herself, and her eyes kept darting towards the untouched plate of sandwiches. Linda gave a sigh of frustration. *Had they all just been sitting there looking at them? Did she have to do everything?* She pushed the plate closer.

"Go on, eat."

The girl snatched a sandwich and took a huge bite, her eyes closing in momentary bliss.

"What's your name?"

The girl looked at Linda uncomprehending.

"Name?"

She muttered something through a mouthful of sandwich—something which sounded like Alina.

"Alina? Is that, Russian?" The girl looked blank again. Linda sighed. "Ruski?" she tried.

The girl shook her head.

"Ukrayinska" she mumbled, taking a second sandwich.

Just then Frankie opened the door to check on them, and Alina froze, shrinking away from him.

"He's OK honey," placated Linda, holding a hand out to reassure her. Then her eyes lit up, and she got to her feet. "I've had an idea, Frankie. I just need to make a quick call," and with that, she darted out of the room, leaving him standing awkwardly in the doorway facing the petrified girl. Frankie gave her a tight smile and strode back into the kitchen.

"Get back in there and make sure she's not stealing anything," he muttered to the twins.

Frankie had a headache coming on. The house was full of noise and people, and he'd been up for two days straight. He could do with everyone pissing off and letting him have a kip.

He called the hospital where he'd had a brief conversation with Big Arf. He was weak and in pain but out of danger. Frankie was glad the big guy had pulled through. He didn't want any more funerals to go to. He sighed and rolled his shoulders. He might just close his eyes for five minutes after all; everything seemed to be under control.

Linda's brainwave had been to ring the woman who did her nails, who was also Ukrainian, and it had been a good call. Once the girl had someone she could speak to, the whole sorry story came out – how she'd been promised a better life in this country. She'd come over here to work as a nanny, but the Albanians had taken her papers along with everything she owned. They had put her to work in the brothel to pay off extra expenses supposedly incurred on her journey, hardly feeding her and promising retaliation on her family back home if she tried to run. She'd been drugged and isolated. Unable to speak more than a few words of English and frightened of reprisals, she was trapped. She didn't know how long it had been since she'd arrived, a few months maybe. But that time had been hell on earth.

By the time Frankie woke from his doze, the house was quiet. He found Chris drinking a cup of tea in the kitchen.

"What did I miss?" he said, voice gravelly with sleep. He ran a hand through his hair, making it stick up wildly.

Chris smiled. "Not much. The girl's gone home with the manicurist who said she could stay with her. That way the gang don't know where she's gone and can't try and snatch her back." He pulled a face, not sure that Frankie was going to like the next part.

"What?"

"Linda's promised the girl that you'll get her passport back from the Albanians. She says after all the girl was a gift; therefore, you get to keep her, and there's no way she's letting her go back there. She wants you to tell them it's part of the peace treaty."

Frankie sighed. They probably only sent the girl for a few hours, but if he was honest, he didn't want to send her back there either. Besides, he knew Linda would make his life hell if he did, and the Albanians were in no position to argue.

43
SCISSORS & SIRENS

Pandora frowned at her reflection. Her wet hair was slicked back, her face apprehensive.

"Darling," purred the hairdresser, "Don't look so worried. This is what I do! Besides, with that face, you could carry anything off. You're going to look sensational!"

She'd barely seen Barclay since her arrival in America. Henri hadn't been kidding when he'd said the man was a consummate workaholic. During one of the brief times she'd seen him he'd told her she needed a rebrand, to shake off the sex bomb image if she was going to make a real splash in Hollywood. She needed to look edgier, more credible.

That had stung. She'd worked hard on her image, and it was because of that she'd got noticed by the papers and landed the parts she had. But he was probably right. After all, he knew his stuff, and this wasn't just about getting noticed, it was about taking her career to the next level. She had to trust him on this.

He'd left the details of a hairdresser by the bedside this

morning, with a note saying they were expecting her at 10am.

The scissors snicked, and as her platinum locks tumbled to the floor, she inhaled then let out a deep breath. This was all part of her new start.

It was hours before she left the salon, and when she did, she was transformed. Gone were the platinum waves, replaced by a much edgier cut, shaved short at the sides and died dark with a blonde-streaked teddy boy quiff at the front. She caught herself in a shop window and paused, startled by her reflection. The extreme haircut emphasised her cheekbones, giving her a fragility. Gone was the sex siren, but if she was honest, this new look made her feel a whole lot more naked than any of her headline-grabbing boob-flashing dresses had. It was just so stripped-back. She had nowhere to hide. And despite herself, she couldn't help thinking that Clay would have hated it.

Pandora glanced at her watch. She was meeting Henri for lunch then had an initial script rehearsal with her acting coach. This was no time to be unsure of herself, and besides, what was done was done.

As she entered the restaurant, Pandora could feel every eye watching her, and not for the usual reasons; she was starting to feel the makeover had been a huge mistake. She stuck her chin in the air and strode towards Henri.

He stood as she approached and began to give a slow clap. *What was he doing? Everyone was turning to look at them!*

She shot him a furious look and hissed "Stop it!" but he just laughed with delight before kissing her cheek.

"I didn't think you'd go through with it!"

She gave a little shrug. "I kind of wish I hadn't."

"Oh nonsense chérie, you look spectacular! It's so much better. Before you were just tits and ass and now you're interesting."

"I'm not sure I want to be interesting."

He laughed. "Of course you do darling!" He lowered his voice, "Have you noticed how many people are taking pictures of us on their phones? Do you think they'd be doing that if they thought you were just another piece of eye candy?" He put his hand over hers. "They want to know who you are. You're still beautiful, but now you're ready to take Hollywood by storm."

Pandora allowed herself a small smile. She hoped he was right. She felt very exposed without her usual platinum mane to hide behind.

Henri waved away her doubts. "Anyway Darling, tell me how you've been getting on with the delicious Barclay?"

"Okay, I suppose," she shrugged, "when I get to see him. But that's only fleetingly when he's on his way in or out of the house."

"Ah, well I'm not surprised. Barclay's obsessed with the work darling, he always has been. Don't take it personally. Between you and me he's a creative leech. You're his current muse, and he's found you the role of a lifetime, but now he's fully immersed in the job. He's got two major projects fighting for attention, and there just isn't room for a grand love affair at the same time."

Pandora frowned, her feelings a little hurt. But if she was honest, she wasn't in love with Barclay either, so it was just her pride that was bruised. Perhaps she was losing her touch; after all, she was used to men going crazy for her. No one had ever been able to take or leave her before, and ambivalence felt pretty crap.

Then again, even she could see that wanting a man to love her just to soothe her ego was pretty selfish, especially when she didn't love him back. Sure they got on well when they actually saw each other, and the sex was fine, but she was under no illusions. It was never going to last forever.

"Look, darling," said Henri, "stop chasing something that isn't there. You'll never capture his total attention, and believe me when I say you don't want to. Accept that you're his inspiration and that he's going to launch you to superstardom. That's more than enough. Come stay with me. I've got more bedrooms than I know what to do with and I could do with the company. We'd have fun. Besides," he gave her a playful nudge, "it would get the paparazzi in a frenzy!"

A smile spread across Pandora's face. Yes, that would be fun. *And it would be nice to be with someone who made no demands on her for a change.*

44
TEA & TOUGH LOVE

Clay lay on his bed watching a fly on the ceiling of his bedroom. He hadn't left his flat in weeks. What was the point? He had no job to go to, and there was no one he wanted to see. He didn't even want to go to the newsagent in case he saw Pandora splashed all over the newspapers again.

His mum had been great. She'd moved herself in and had fed him home-cooked food and put up with his foul temper while he came off the booze. Despite his ranting and self-pity, she'd stuck it out, refusing to put up with any of his shit, and he was gradually adjusting. He was glad she was there. She was the only good thing in his life right now; after all, he'd totally fucked everything else.

He heaved himself upright and put his feet on the floor. He could do with a cup of tea. Nobody made tea like his mum did. That was something Pandora had never got the hang of, but then she couldn't boil an egg either, so perhaps it wasn't surprising. Her talents lay in other areas. He shook his head in frustration. He didn't need to be thinking about her; she made him want a drink.

He found his mum in the kitchen unpacking shopping and gave her a kiss on the cheek.

"Cup of tea love?"

"You're the best," he smiled and plonked himself down in the chair, scratching his hair and yawning.

She smiled indulgently and filled the kettle. While she waited for the water to boil, she leaned back against the work surface, arms folded and looked at her son.

"What?"

"I'm going home today."

Clay felt a mild panic rising but styled it out. "Don't be silly. You don't have to do that."

"Yes Clarence, I do. You've lolled around feeling sorry for yourself for weeks now, and enough is enough. You need to get back on with your life."

He stuck his bottom lip out, reminding her of the seven-year-old version of him. But that only hardened her resolve. He'd regressed to being a kid since she moved in and it was time for him to stand on his own two feet again.

"And when has that face ever worked on me, Clarence?" She said, hands on hips. "So, you're going to get in the shower, get yourself dressed and you're going to go and see Frankie. You apologise for making such a mess of things, and you ask him for a job."

Clay started to protest, but she silenced him with a finger. "I dare say it won't be the fancy-schmancy job you had before, but you need to keep busy. Sitting around in your pyjamas all day being waited on hand and foot isn't going to get you back on your feet."

Clay blew out his cheeks and let out a long breath. He didn't much fancy facing Frankie, but he supposed he'd have to do it sooner or later.

"I'll do it tomorrow. Can't you stay for one more day?"

"No, Clarence," she said, her tone brokering no argument. "You get off your backside and do it today. No more sitting on your arse."

"Yes, mum."

She nodded curtly, pleased. "Good. Cos I've already told him you're coming."

She poured the tea and Clay rolled his eyes, throwing his head back in a mock scream, but he quickly fixed his expression before she turned back around.

She set the steaming mug of tea in front of him and slid a hand over his.

"Look, son. Nobody loves you like I do, which is why I'm giving you a kick up the bum. That girl was bad news and the last thing you needed. You need to put her out of your head and knuckle down to some old-fashioned hard work. You let Frankie down, and you need to put in some hard graft to regain his trust. You concentrate on that and make sure you keep off the booze, yes?"

He nodded.

"And when the time is right, you'll meet a nice girl, and things will work out. But you need to sort yourself out first. I've started you off, but the rest has to be up to you."

Clay took a sip of tea, his hands wrapped around the comforting warmth of the mug. His heart thumped at the thought of seeing Frankie. He'd got used to being isolated in his own little world but he had no option now his mum had stuck her oar in. He was going to have to bite the bullet and make amends.

Clay was right to be nervous about seeing Frankie. It wasn't a comfortable meeting. Frankie was not a man who forgot being let down, and Clay was forced to recognise for the first time just how badly he'd screwed things up.

For a while, Frankie had even let him think he was going to cut him loose, but eventually, he'd relented.

It wasn't getting his old job back, not by a long stretch, but it was work, and that was what he needed right now. With his mum gone he'd go crazy in the flat alone all day, and being busy was the best way to quiet the call of the bottle and dull his aching heart.

The worst part about the new job would be reporting

to Chris, something he would never have stood for a few months ago, but now he wasn't so bothered. Chris had kept his nose clean, proved himself loyal and been rewarded for it. *Fair enough.* Clay needed to concentrate on getting his life back on track.

He took a long slow walk home after meeting Frankie. He'd been cooped up in his flat for too long, and it felt good to be outside. The sun was shining, but the air still had a crisp nip to remind him it wasn't quite spring yet. He shoved his hands deep into his pockets and took a deep breath.

As he rounded the next corner, he did a double-take. There was a woman pushing a pram further up the street, and he could have sworn it was Ivy. He snorted to himself. *What were the odds of that?* He was seeing ghosts of the past everywhere.

Strangely one of Frankie's conditions for taking him back had been that he didn't contact Ivy. He thought it was an odd stipulation, after all, he hadn't seen her in months, but he'd agreed. Ivy wouldn't want to see him anyway. It wasn't as if they parted on good terms. He squinted at the figure receding into the distance, trying to work out if it was her. She must have met someone and settled down, maybe that was why Frankie didn't want him stirring up trouble for her.

Clay slowed, not wanting her to sense he was there and watched her until she went out of sight. Then he turned and walked in the opposite direction. He wasn't going to disobey Frankie. He smiled sadly to himself. At least Ivy had found happiness.

45
DEATH & DIVORCE

Clay's new job was as a courier, and while it wasn't glamorous or exciting, it certainly kept him busy. He kept himself to himself, worked hard, and found that by the time he got home of an evening, he was too tired to do anything other than watch some telly and grab a bite to eat.

His mum had given him a beginner's cookbook since he wouldn't have the spare cash to buy takeaways, and he was slowly getting the hang of cooking for himself. He was even starting to enjoy the simple satisfaction of having eaten something he'd made himself that wasn't a piece of toast or a microwave meal. Plus, it gave him something to do when he got home. All the other lads headed down the pub, but he didn't feel ready for that, so he kept his head down and stayed on the straight and narrow.

It was about three weeks later when he returned from work to find divorce papers sitting on his doormat. He should have known this day would come, but after the initial shock, he was surprised by his own lack of reaction.

He'd done a lot of thinking while on his daily delivery runs. And while he'd loved Pandora, he was starting to see how toxic their marriage had been. They were doomed from the start. They had always wanted different things so it could never have worked.

So, instead of reaching for a bottle, he made himself a cuppa and sat down at the kitchen table. He read the divorce papers from start to finish, occasionally having to look words up to make sure he understood them. She was citing his unreasonable behaviour as the reason for the divorce, which was fair enough. He had been pretty damn unreasonable and drunk and controlling.

Once read, he signed the papers, sealed the envelope and decided to post them straight away. Better to draw a line under the whole thing. Then he'd treat himself to fish and chips to celebrate being young, free and single. Plus, he hadn't had a takeaway in ages, and everyone knew Frankie's fish and chips were the best in town.

There was a queue in The Codfather, but that was to be expected on a Friday night. Everyone wanted a treat at the end of the working week.

Clay waited quietly in a world of his own, thinking about Pandora and the mess he'd made of things. He'd do things so differently if he had his choices again. When he finally got to the front of the queue, he looked up and was surprised to find himself staring into Ivy's startled eyes. Her hair was back to the familiar auburn, and she looked great if rather cross.

They looked at one another. After a few seconds, Clay found his voice.

"Hey," he said, feeling foolish. "I didn't know you worked in here." His voice sounded croaky, and he winced.

Her mouth set in a hard line. "What can I get you?"

He couldn't blame her for being angry. He'd acted like a prize twat after all.

"Cod and chips please."

She served him, putting his steaming paper-wrapped

parcel down on the counter and moved onto the next customer, without meeting his eyes. He stood for a moment watching her work. But he couldn't think what to say, and she was already busy with the jostling queue of hungry customers. He took the food and with his head full of jumbled thoughts and regrets he walked back home, Frankie's warning ringing in his ears.

There was no vinegar on the chips. She hadn't asked, and he hadn't hung around to add any himself, he'd been too thrown by the encounter. He would never have gone in if he'd known Ivy worked there, but now he'd seen her he was taken aback by her response. He hadn't expected such anger. She'd always been so easy-going, she'd never been cross with him. Was she still angry about him firing her? That would be fair enough.

His stomach lurched as an alternative occurred to him. Had he done something else while he was drinking and he couldn't remember? He racked his brain, trying to think of what he could have done, but there were whole evenings that were blank no matter how hard he searched his memory. He had no idea what he'd done or said since the drinking had started in earnest. Unfairly sacking her was bad enough, he hoped he hadn't done even worse.

His mind had kept returning to Ivy ever since seeing her with the pram, but he kept pushing thoughts of her away, especially after Frankie's warning. Knowing she was happy out there was one thing, but he couldn't stand thinking he'd done something to make her hate him.

He considered going to see her, and his stomach turned over. *It's only Ivy for Christ's sake.*

But perhaps that was the problem. She wasn't only Ivy. It was just that he hadn't realised that before. And he couldn't bear the thought of her despising him. Even now she was happy with someone else and had a family of her own he desperately wanted to clear the air.

He had to go and try to make things right. No matter

what he'd promised Frankie, and no matter the cost.

46
ENDINGS & BEGINNINGS

On Saturday morning, Ivy's mum was in town shopping, so Ivy had the house to herself. The baby was asleep, and she was enjoying a well-deserved half an hour of peace and quiet when the doorbell rang.

She winced and glanced over at the crib, but the baby didn't stir. She dashed to the door before whoever it was could ring again. All she wanted was another ten minutes of peace.

So when she opened the door, she was already frowning, and her frown deepened further when she saw Clay standing on the doorstep. He stood there, seemingly dumbstruck. Ivy wondered for a minute whether she'd forgotten something crucial. Was she still wearing her pyjamas? Had she got jam smeared across her face or baby sick down her top? She glanced down and reassured herself that everything was fine. He still hadn't said anything. Ivy crossed her arms, waiting, her expression impatient. After all, he'd come to her front door.

Clay stared at Ivy, his heart thumping. She looked beautiful, fresh-faced. And really pissed off.

Finally, she got fed up of waiting for him to say something.

"What are you doing here?"

"I didn't expect you to be here; I thought your mum would answer."

The corner of her mouth twitched. *Christ, was Clay actually nervous?* At seeing her? That wasn't like him at all. She nearly laughed but then held firm. Why should she make this any easier for him?

"What are you talking about Clarence?"

He cringed at the use of his full name. He knew she was angry if she was calling him that.

"I just thought…" he said, and stopped, running a hand through his hair. This wasn't turning out the way he'd planned at all. "Well, I expected your mum to answer."

Her eyebrows shot up, and she wondered if he'd gone mad.

"Oh well if it's mum you came to see you'll have to come back later, she's in town."

Clay closed his eyes and took a breath. "That's not what I meant. I saw you out with a baby a few weeks ago, and I assumed you'd moved into a place of your own."

She didn't reply.

"Congratulations?" he said, risking a smile.

In the background, the baby started to whimper. Ivy looked over her shoulder, then back at Clay before starting to close the door. "Look, I've really got to go."

Clay shoved his foot in the gap to stop her, earning himself a stern look.

"Please Ivy. I just wanted to say sorry. I treated you badly, and I know you're happy with someone else now, but please let me apologise."

She gave a huff and went into the living room to pick up the crying baby, leaving the door ajar. Clay waited on the doorstep.

Shushing the baby, Ivy glanced back at him then gave a

sigh. "Come in then; you can stick the kettle on."

Clay stepped inside the house, a house that he'd been in so many times before, a house he felt comfortable in. It was like a blanket being put around his shoulders. He hadn't realised how much he'd missed this, how much he'd missed her.

He stood at the kitchen sink and filled the kettle. What had he been thinking? He'd been dazzled by Pandora and hadn't seen what had been right in front of him all along. And now he'd missed his chance.

Ivy stood, cradling the baby, and as Clay watched her, his heart dropped through the floor. She was beautiful, her face radiant as she gazed down at her child. He hesitated, not wanting to mess up when he was already on such shaky ground. The baby was dressed in blue, so surely must be a boy?

He peered down at the little face.

"Hello, little fella," then turned to Ivy, "Can I hold him?"

She gave Clay a sideways look. "Really?"

His face fell, and she relented. "Sit down, and mind you support his head," she said and passed the baby gently over to him.

Clay took the precious bundle and sat, staring down at the little face. The baby quieted and stared back with bright blue eyes the same colour as Clay's own. Ivy's face softened, it was good to see the two of them together.

"He's beautiful," Clay said, a huge grin spreading across his face, "just like his mum."

He was pleased that things had worked out so well for Ivy, but he felt a pang of sadness. How had he got things so wrong?

Ivy took a sip of tea as she watched the two of them. There wasn't much to say. She knew everything had gone wrong between him and Pandora. She knew about the drinking and that he'd hit rock bottom. Her mum had revelled in giving her all the gossip. She'd meant it as a cautionary tale.

But despite everything Ivy felt desperately sorry for him. She'd almost been tempted to reach out, but she'd stopped herself when she thought of the baby. Her baby came first now. Gone were the days of dropping everything for Clay.

And besides, he seemed to be under the impression she'd met someone else. He had no idea the baby was his, and that suited her just fine. It wouldn't do him any harm at all to think she was happy without him. He didn't realise she was living here with her mum raising the baby between them.

The last thing she wanted was pity or a sense of obligation from him. He could stuff that idea.

A little fist waved and caught Clay in the face. He chuckled.

"He's going to be a right bruiser this one isn't he?" and he paused, unable to resist fishing for information about the guy who had everything he'd always wanted.

"Is his dad handy with his fists too?"

Ivy rolled her eyes and chuckled.

"You could say that," she smiled.

THE END

OTHER TITLES BY TM THORNE

FRANKIE FINCH BOOKS

Notorious:
Danger, Deception, Desire

Accused:
Stardom, Scandal, Survival

Driven:
Racing, Rivalry Revenge

Caged:
Rock, Ransom, Retribution

Made:
The Frankie Finch prequel (short story)

THE LONDON VAMPIRE SERIES

Spooked

Jinxed

Enthralled (short story)

Printed in Great Britain
by Amazon